Insomnia

Alec Joen

Contents

1-The wedding.

Sophia POV

I can't believe she's making me go to her own wedding!! My mother is getting married, how many kids could say they went to their parent wedding, well apparently I can.

The name is Sophia, I'm sixteen and it feels like my life just ended. My mother who was a single mother her whole life decided that she had enough with the single life and want to get married, yeyy her.

I wasn't against her having a life or getting laid, god knows she need it. I'm objecting to me being dragged around the country.

I'm a city girl, I'm born and raised and LA, I can't do country, forest doesn't appeal me, I don't even like the snow. Okay I never saw it before, but doesn't mean I'm missing much.

Today is the cursed day, today is her wedding, I hardly knew her new husband, it was love from first sight.

She told me it was made to be, and she tell me not to rush into getting a boyfriend and still she'll marry someone she just met.

If that wasn't the worst part, then this must be it. He have five kids, five sons to be exact. I'm used to having my own bathroom and not sharing how am I supposed to live with five step brothers.

Not one, not two but five!! Their youngest is fourteen, meaning they are all teenagers. God, why is life so cruel on my poor soul.

Mom wasn't gonna wear a big white dress, just a simple sundress one, she had some light make up on and she looked beautiful.

She have long jet black hair, brown eyes and a heart shaped face. I on the other hand had my looks from my dad her Highschool sweetheart. My hair is practically white, no I'm not into the silver trend it's how i was born. My eyes are hazel colour and I'm too pale compared to her olive skin that's look tanned and healty.

Thankfully mum never hated me for looking like him, she never called me a mistake or a fault, she loved me. I'm mommy's little girl or at least I used to be, as I grew older people would think we are friends never mother and daughter which is okay with me.

My mom is my only friend, she's my secret keepers even my embarrassing ones. When I get too scared or stressed I'll go to little space to help me, my little age is about three maybe four depend. I never regress too much, and momma never hated me for it, she took care of me even then.

Now that we're moving, did I mention that we're moving? Let me say it again we are FUCKING MOVING across the country, I don't think I'll be able to be little me again.

The new town we're heading to isn't LA, there everyone know each other. The school is simple two buildings, everyone been together since kinder-garten.

And here I come the new girl, I hate being new, I might not look like this but I'm really shy. Especially around new people, and new faces.

"Sophia time to go" my mum yelled from downstairs, I could hear how happy she is.

I'm only doing this for her, once I hit eighteen I'm back to LA and to my life.

I did a last check on the room before I leave, everything was set in boxes and went into the van. Everything except my personal items, my Ipad, phone, charger, earphones and of course my teddy bear. He'll be scared to sit alone in a van the whole way there.

I got him into my backpack and left the room saying goodbye to my old and only bedroom.

I went downstairs and got in the car with Fredrik, my new step father. It's just him, mom and I. We have an appointment at the church for them to be married then we're off the road to our new home.

I'm dressed for the occasion in a baby blue sun dress and some flats, I can't walk in heals to save my life. Even Fredrik was dressed in some jeans and a button up shirt, his tattoos were showing all over his hand and neck.

Who knew my mom would go for the tattooed bad looking guy, but I'll give it to her even for a guy in his forties he's in a very good shape with strong muscles.

He's also twice my height, mom is taller then me by few inches but him, I hardly touch his chest. I still got two years to gain some height or so my doctor says.

The ceremony were fast and straight to the point, I announce you husband and wife, they didn't even get to the part of kissing the bride, we just left.

I got in the back of the SUV, and put my earphones on, music on, world off.

I must have dosed for a bit since i was shaken awake by my mother, did we make it already?

We got into a restaurant for early dinner since we'll be driving through the night. I didn't appreciate my nap being cut short so i was grumpy while in the restaurant.

Nothing looked to be appealing for me so I just shrugged and let my new "dad" to choose for me.

I nibbled a bit at my food and drank my pepsi, until they were finally done and we could leave.

"You hardly ate anything Soph" Fredrik comment.

"Not hungry' I just mumble. "It's a long way home" he warn me and I just shrug.

We get back in the car and I fall asleep again with my earphones on.

I was actually comfortable in the silent car, having nice dreams until I felt us stop.

There was car door opening and closing and then some murmur.

Finally i was picked out of the car by some strong hands probably Fred, for some reason he sniffed me and growled. I must be dreaming, right?

2-Brothers.

Sophia POV

I wole up in a strange bed, looking around I didn't recognize my surroundings where am I?

I wasn't in my sundress either, I had on an oversized T-shirt. It wasn't even mine, in my hand was my pink teddy Mr.sparkle.

I jumped out of the bed and frankly looked around, someone tucked me in bed and even gave me my teddy bear.

Please god tell me it was mom who did all this. On further inspections i found most of my boxes from home inside the room, so this must be my new room.

It was a giant room compared to the one back at home, it even had an ensuit bathroom! I don't have to share, i went and washed my face and teeth, did my buisness. Then searched between the boxes for my clothes, i couldn't find any shirt so i just added some yoga pants underneath the shirt, it's large enough to be a dress on me.

I left the room and saw several doors closed, most of them had some decoration on them. I went downstairs hoping to find my mother, she's a coffeeholic, so I'm hoping to find her in the kitchen making her coffee.

Few wrong turns here and there and I found the kitchen, it's was also one hell of a kitchen, it was the size of our old apartment. We're living in a mansion now, I guess.

Mom was there as expected, I ran and gave her a hug, waking up in new place is scary, I was trying my best not to go to my little space.

"Good morning princess" mom said in her forever happy voice.

"Morning mommy" I reply in a whisper.

"Someone isn't feeling very big today?" she asks and I nod still hiding in her arms

"It's okay baby, I know you're scared but it's okay" she said while petting my hair.

I heard a throat being clenaed and turned around to see Fredrik.

"Good morning soph" he said with a smile.

"Morning" I reply hardly a mumble.

He eyes my shirt choice and smile before turning to make a cup of coffee of his own.

"You ready to meet your new brothers?" he asks me again and I shrug, I was hoping not to see them, but i guess it's a must.

Mom took a seat at the breakfast bar with Fredrik next to her, I guess I should get used to sharing her.

I sat down too and Fred offered me a cup of orange juice. The first boy to come in the kitchen was one who looked young, younger then me even, he was dressed in a T-shirt and his boxers only.

"Sam" his father scolds once he saw the attire.

"Morning to you too father" sam replies in a voice filled with sarcasm.

"Get dressed, we have girls that live with us now"

"Well she's my new mom and she got you" he said pointing at mum shrugging while he went to pour a glass of juice for him.

"Sophia this is Samuel, he's your new younger brother" Fred introduce us.

"Welcome to the family sis" sam replies cheering me with his orange juice before he left the kitchen hopefully to get dressed.

Next to come in where two guys one really look like Fred with his brown hair and brown eyes while the other had green eyes. They were as tall as Fred and even had some tattoos like him.

"These are Alvin and Adam, Alvin is twenty while Adam is seventeen" he introdcue them.

They both eye my shirt with a smirk and then share a look like a private conversation between them and finally they break into a laugh.

They don't know me yet and already are laughing at me, I felt tears gather in my eyes. I just want to leave already, I looked for a way to leave the kitchen unnoticed.

Another guy walked in the kitchen this one looked like Adam, same green eyes, same tattoos. He saw my teary face and i looked away hiding all evidence. He slapped both of the laughing hyenas back head and pointed toward me.

They stopped laughing instantly, he turned back to me and offered me a big warm smile.

"I'm Victor, that idiot is my twin" he says confirming my suspicion about how similar they look.

"We're so happy to have you in the family, what's your name baby girl?" he ask in a smooth voice that's filled with dominance.

"Sophia" I whisper but still he heard it.

"Sophia" he says it again, excpet it sounded like he was tasting the word not simply saying it.

"Always wanted a sis, welcome to the family" Adam says giving me a hug, I heard a low growl before he let me go but I guess I was imagining.

"Welcome to the family" Alvin says keeping his distance.

"Where's Kyle?" Fred asks his sons.

"Still asleep probably" Alvin replies.

"Kyle is same age as you soph, he'll be with you tomorrow in school as will the twins and Sammy" Fred tell me.

Wow, I'll have four of my brothers with me in school, well at least I won't be alone for the first day.

"Now who want breakfast" Fred asks taking me out of my thoughts.

We all shouted me, there was even two muffles shouts from upstairs. .

I ended up sitting next to Sammy and Victor at breakfast. Everyone kept eyeing me, like I they knew something and I don't. Weird...

3-Family.

S ophia POV.

I won't be going to school until tomorrow, that means I have a full day to get used to everything and everyone.

I met the mysterious Kyle during breakfast, we was sixteen like me. He's cute and funny and he welcomed me with a big twirl making me giggle but Victor snatched me out of his hands saying he might drop me.

They've hardly knew me for few hours and they are already being possessive and worried about me.

Maybe having brothers won't be so bad, they gave me a house tour, the boys all have a room of their own beside mine. My mother and step father room is on the second floor.

They had an entertainment room or a man cave to exact. It had a bar, pool table, a plasma TV, PlayStation set up.

The backyard of the house was enormous and blends in with the forest.

"Just don't go to the forest alone little sis" Alvin warn me.

I noticed that Alvin might be the oldest and they all listen to him but they also listen to Victor, even Alvin did what Victor asked question free.

I never had any sibling and so i didn't really understand their dynamic. They had stake for dinner while mum who knew I don't do big chunks of meat, she made chicken nuggets for me. It was that or she'll have to cut it for me, I didn't need my mum to cut my food infront of my new step father and brothers.

I was kind of embarrassed, eating differently then the rest, but still better from the other option.

"You don't like steak?" kyle asked with disbelief.

I just shrugged avoiding an answer, I ate my dinner in silence while they talked about school and what not.

After dinner I was excused from helping with cleaning and sent to bed so I can rest for tomorrow.

I headed to my room and changed to my own pyjamas, I hugged my teddy Mr.sparkle close and went to sleep.

I was about to sleep when there was a knock on the door, I went to open the door and saw Sammy.

"Uhhh...just came to say goodnight to my new sister" he says with a blush, he looked adorable and he's the only little brother I'll ever get so why not. I gave sam a hug and a kiss.

I was about to go back to my room when kyle passed by, he too got a kiss and hug.

"Ohh do i get to kiss my new sister too" Adam asked with a smirk, while Victor just stood there smiling at us.

I gave the twins their share of kisses and hugs, well since i already hugged every one. I ran toward Alvin bedroom, he was surprised to see me and even more shocked when I gave him a hug.

"Apparently we all get hug and kisses before bed from now on." Victor said from behind me.

His words made me blush, I just escaped back to my room and went to bed. I slept easily and only woke up to my alarm the next morning.

Now starting a new school is going to be hard wether I had my new brothers with me or not.

I did my morning routine and then went to chose my clothes, first impression are important. I didn't really know what to wear and spend several minutes just searching through my wardrobe.

I decided on my high waisted jeans with a pink T-shirt and my tennis shoes. I let my white hair down and did my very quick make up routine, mascara and lip gloss done.

I got my backpack and moved to the kitchen. My brothers were all there having breakfast, my stomach was in too much torment to accept any food so I just moved my food around waiting till it's time to go.

"Sophia eat baby" Victor was the one to notice I haven't eat anything.

"Mhmmm" I reply still not feeling like i can eat.

Victor got up and got me a glass of orange juice, well at least I think i can drink that.

"I'm taking sophie with me, Adam can drive you two" Victor said before picking my backpack up and offering me a hand.

We went to the garage and i see a variation of cars, and trucks. Victor skip them all and go toward a shiny silver motorcycle.

"Ever been on one?" he asks and i shake my head no.

"All you have to do is hold to me" he says before getting a helmet, he place it over my head and it's a little big, he had to adjust the straps of it.

"I'll need to get you a smaller size helmet" he mumble to himself.

He got on first and then helped me get up behind him, I placed my arms on his side but he took both hands and made me hug him even closer.

He turned the bike on and took off slowly first before he added some speed, I hugged him even closer.

"You scared of the speed?" he asks slowing down.

"A little" i confess.

He drove the rest of the way in a slower pace for me, once we made it to school, he parked his motorcycle and got down.

He helped me on to my feets and took the helmet off, he even fixed my hair for me.

He was looking at me weirdly, in a look full of love and care. I just shrugged it out and let him take me toward the office.

"Good morning Victor" the lady says. "Good morning, I'm here to get my sister schedule" he says and I'm grateful I don't like talking to strangers.

"Name sugar?" she asks me and I mumble sophia but it wasn't enough.

"Her name is Sophia Nightshade" he says giving me the same last name as theirs instead of my mother's.

She hand him the schedule and he thank her before walking us out of the office.

4-School.

Sophia POV.

After we, well Victor got my schedule we walked outside and back to the parking lot. Adam just parked his jeep and got out along with kyle and Sam.

Sammy said he'll go to see his friends wishing me luck on my first day. My schedule was handed to Kyle who just laughs before handing it to me.

"What's funny?" I ask curiously. "We have the same schedule little sis," Kyle says with evil glee.

"Get her in trouble and I'm kicking your ass" Victor warns.

"Me??Neverrrr!" Kyle replies faking innocence making me giggle.

"Don't look at me, I'll hold you down while he kicks your ass" Adam says giving me a wink.

"Get her to class" he orders Kyle handing him my backpack. Before turning toward me.

"I'll see you at lunch baby girl" he kissed the top of my head before leaving with Adam.

Kyle took my hand and walked us to the first class, he seriously knew everyone since he said hello to way too many people, I felt like hiding behind his back several times. I couldn't go little in school, that would be really embarrassing.

We finally made it to our class, Kyle, of course, went to sit with his friends, they were all big guys with buff muscles, not as much as my new brother but still intimidating.

"I can sit alone?"It came out more like a question to Kyle.

He was about to say no, I saw it in his eyes but I gave him my best puppy eyes, and he sighs and hands me my backpack. I don't sit in the front, I prefer a seat closer to the window, away from most of the class.

A girl with black hair and black eyes sat next to me, even her skin was the complete opposite of me, we looked like ying and yang making me giggle.

I place both hands on my mouth, hiding my giggles, but it was too late she looks at me, probably hearing my giggle. Now she'll hate me or think I'm making fun of her.

"Love your hair," she says in a nice voice, for a second I thought she must be joking or being mean so I stay quiet.

"I'm Niti, you must be new," she says again with a gentle smile, maybe she isn't making fun of me.

"I'm Sophia" I reply blushing, why am I blushing. Damn my shyness.

"Nice meeting you soph," she says again and I relax. Okay, she's nice, I give her that.

The class began and I had to pay attention, some people eyed me weird, but I did my best to ignore them.

After the bell ring I got up and got my backpack and got ready to leave for the next.

"I got history next what about you?" Niti asks.

"Me too" I say shyly and she smile at me again.

Kyle came toward us, he greeted Niti, of course he know her too, he tried to take my bag but I kept it on.

"We can go to class alone Kyle" I say. "Can't do, boss order to stay with you" he says before he placed a hand around me and the other around Niti.

Almost half the school eyes us while walking, I felt like crying now.

Kyle on the other hand kept nodding and smiling to everyone, who's his boss, I need to file a complain.

We walked in the next class and we took a seat far away from my new brother. He acted the same until it was time for lunch and I had enough, I told my new friend that we need to get away from him.

"Sure, it would be fun" she said with a small laugh.

When the bell rang, we took off without him while he was busy with his friends.

We ran through the hallways laughing, she was write this is fun. I didn't have much friends in LA, and the one I had we definitely didn't run around the hallways avoiding my new step-brother.

I was too busy laughing and trying to catch my breath when I hit a wall, Aouch, should watch where I'm going.

"You okay Sophia?" the wall asks.

I look up and it wasn't a wall, it was my other step-brother, now i wasn't sure if this is Victor or Adam. I still had hard time knowing whom is whom between them.

"Yeah I'm fine" I reply taking his offered hand to help me up.

"Victor" Niti says bowing her head a little, so it's Victor who I stumbled up with. He nodded back to her before turning to me.

"What got you running like this baby girl?" he asks and the nickname make me wanna go to my little self so badly but I resist.

"Uhhh...we're hiding from Kyle" i tell him truthfully.

"And can I know why?" he asks raising an eyebrow.

I just shrug, I couldn't take being walked by Kyle for another second.

"Come on let's get you some lunch" Victor says offering me a hand.

We walk to the cafeteria and all eyes are on us again, I couldn't help but hide behind him this time, I didn't like all this attention.

"It's okay baby girl" again with the same nickname making me feel small.

"Why don't you go sit down and I'll get you lunch?" he asks and I nod yes, anything to get away from the center of attention.

He point me toward a table where Adam must be sitting, along with a red looking Kyle.

I dragged Niti along with me before taking a seat.

"That wasn't nice little sister" Kyle scold the second I sit down.

"Sowwwyyy..." I say slipping before covering my mouth and looking down embarrassed.

"Hey it's okay, just don't do it again" Kyle says offering me a smile.

I smile back too, Victor got both me and Niti lunch along with his own. I had a deal with Kyle that he'll just hold my hand from now on and I won't run away again, although it was fun.

5-Thunder-Storm.

Victor POV.

Wolves only found their mate once, my father only found his late in life after he got all five of us. He thought he'll never find her, most wolves do at a young age, our mates are always close to us, it's how the goddess created us.

But on a business trip that he wasn't even expecting to go on, he saw her, she had a daughter but it was okay with us. She's our father true mate and the only one to make his wolf happy.

The day she moved in, she moved in along with the last person i expected her to bring, My Mate. Her daughter is my mate, I always thought that my mate won't show up until I'm much older like my father.

But she did, when the car door opened and her smell hit me, I couldn't resist but picking her up and smelling her. The smell of honey and roses, like heaven to my wolf.

I carried her to the room we had ready for her, it was close to mine, if I knew she would be mine then I would prepared a place for her with me.

I knew from my father that her mother was halfbreed only, her father was human. That means my mate have some wolfblood in her, not enough to make her shift but still she have enough of it in her to give her a mate.

She didn't know anything about wolves or mates and i won't scare her right away with everything. I wanted to take things slow, my wolf, was too possessive for my plan.

When we took her to her bedroom i dressed her in my shirt, making her smell like me.

I left her bedroom and went to mine were my brothers were waiting for me.

"So our sister?" Adam my twin ask. "She's my mate" i tell them.

There was a chorus of congratulations and hugs, I was the first to find his mate between all five of us.

"So what's the gam plan?" Kyle asks, impatient as always.

"Nothing, treat her as your sister" I tell them, warning them to be nice with her.

"Of course she was our sister since she's father's mate daughter, but now she's more then a step-sister. She's family" Alvin our oldest and my beta says.

Although he's older then me, and Adam is my twin I'm still the strongest between them, my father is the current alpha and I'm next in line.

"I can't believe I'm getting an older sister...like if you guys don't boss me around enough" Sammy our youngest says with a pout.

"What about you being a daddy" my twin Adam asks, he's right I am a daddy, they all knew it.

But none of us know how the girl would feel about it, will she hate me for it, would she like it. Would she be scared from the idea of being my baby or would she enjoy it, all the ideas where going through my mind.

"Don't worry man she was made for you" Alvin assures me.

The next morning we officially our new sister and my mate, her name is Sophia, even her name was beautiful.

The first few days were just getting to know each others, I tried to study her. She blushes easily, she slipped with her words few times, even hide behind me when there are too many eyes on her.

I also noticed few habits she had while eating, she doesn't like steak but I also noticed she's never given a knife. Her food is usually cut for her or she'll get something with smaller bite size.

On her first night with us, Sammy went to say good night to her, she's adorable enough that he didn't care if he get bossed by her too.

She eneded up giving hugs and kisses to the whole fam, as long as I got my hug and no one hugged her for too long I was okay with it.

Tonight she didn't seem to be herself, she was lost in her own ideas. When it was time for us to head to bed she didn't give us the hugs and kisses we were getting used to, instead she went straight to her room.

There was a thunder storm, it's very usual for us, I just hoped the sound won't wake her up. I went to bed thinking about her and why she's so sad tonight, we go to school together and i have Kyle keepin an eye on her, nothing happened or he would've told me.

I closed to my eyes and went to sleep, I heard thunder then a muffled scream. Being a werewolf and an alpha I heard the voice loudly and clearly even muffled.

I left my bedroom and headed toward the source of the voice, Sophia's room. I knocked on the door lightly before going in, I saw her lights on and she had the blanket up to her chin, her eyes were shut close.

Another thunder and she scream again, she's scared of the thunder.

I walk toward her slowly not to scare her, she must heard me come in, on closer inspection I saw tears going down her face.

"Sophia" I whisper my heart breaking for the sight. She scream again scared.

"Shh...shhh It's just me, just me, Victor" I tell her and she stop screaming, only the tears going down now.

"I didn't mean to scare you I just wanted to check on you" I tell her.

"I'm fine" she says in a broken voice.

I was about to argue when another thunder sounded and she screamed again, I couldn't leave her alone like this.

"Move Sophia" I tell her and she look at me like i just grew a second head.

"Come on move" i say in my daddy voice and she obeys. I got in bed next to her and pulled her close to me, her head nestled on my chest.

"Now I'm here you can sleep baby girl" I say kissing the top of her head.

She snuggle closer, I noticed she had her teddy too, but she was trying to hide him.

I almost forgot about him, I found it in her bag when she first arrived and placed it with her in bed, I wasn't sure if she sleep with him or if it's just a childhood token.

I pulled the teddy from under the covers and gave it to her so she can hug him properly. She looked at me with wide eyes and i just smiled, now i knew for sure she's going to be my little princess.

6-Girls Talk.

Sophia POV.

I hate thunder storms, always had always will. Usually I'll sleep with my mother whenever there is one but now she's married, I can't go sleep between her and her new husband.

In time like those I wish I had a daddy, someone who would hug me and keep me safe. I went to bed dredging the night to come, every time the thunder will go I would scream, I tried to cover my mouth so I won't wake up my new brothers.

I even left the light on since I hated the dark too, around midnight I heard a knock but knew I was imagining, no one would come to my roon at night. I closed my eyes and tried not to imagine the serial killer coming to end me when I heard my name being called and I screamed scared.

It wasn't a serial killer, it was my brother, how embarrassing is it, to have your new step-brother find out what a scarry cat i am.

Instead he made me move so he can sleep next to me, I had Mr.sparkle in my arms, he'll be scared to sleep alone too. I tried to keep him hidden but Victor pulled him up into my arms and told me to sleep.

I never slept next to a guy before, the only time i actually hugged a guy was with my new step-brothers. I loved how they were all more buff then me and could hide the whole of me in their bear hugs.

But sleeping next to Victor felt different, I felt safe and very little next to him. I felt my thumb move up to my mouth and i began to suck on it, a habbit of mine while in little space.

I fell asleep with him there keeping me safe from the thunder. I didn't know how weird it would be to make your step-brother sleep next to you while you sucked on your thumb and hugged your teddy until the morning.

He was simply smiling down at me while I blushed as red as a tomato. I removed my thumb from my mouth right away embarrassed as hell now.

"Good morning princess" he says still smiling, was he making fun of me.

"Uhh..ehm...morning Victor" I say not knowing what to do now.

"Come on get up or we'll be late for school" he says before leaving the room and leaving me to get ready.

I ran out of the bed and got dressed in a new record, I need to speak with my mom, right away.

I ran up toward her room only to hear the voice of my other step-brother scolding me.

"Don't run on the stairs Sophia" came Alvin voice.

I slowed down not wanting another remark, his scolding and yesterday events made me want to be my little self even more.

I knock on the door before going in, not wanting to see anything I shouldn't. I hear the word come in and get in running, mum was still in bed, i jump on top of the bed and go hug her.

"Shh what's wrong baby girl?" she asks moving my hair out of my face.

I didn't know i was crying until she wipped my tears away. Why was I crying, I was just, confused and had to let it out.

"Now tell mama what's wrong" she ask in a voice she knew i couldn't say no to.

"Last night there was thunder" I tell her and her face soften, she knew i hate it.

"I'm sorry baby, I left you alone" she says in a sad voice.

"I wasn't alone, uhh...victor slept next to me last night" I say blushing.

"AhhI see..." Mum says."Mum, I...it's....ahhh" I say lost for word.

"Shh it's okay, you're a big girl now and all" she says smiling.

Why is she so okay with that!! And what the hell, Eww.

"Mum he's my brother" I say disgusted, or at least faking it, just a little bit.

"Step brother" she correct me with a wink.

"Aren't you supposed to tell me no?" I ask in disbelief to what i just heard.

She just laugh and shrug, she knew something i didn't. And i know from experience she won't tell me until she's ready.

I was going to demand more answers when the door to their bathroom opened and my step dad stepped out in just his pyjama bottom, his chest was on full display and i saw the different tattoo he had there.

But the one that interested me the most was the name of my mother right over his heart.

Anna was written in black ink, it was readable from even far away, I didn't know if that was cute or too much.

"Like what you see little girl?" Fred ask and i look away embarrassed.

"I never saw so many tattoos, mum never allowed me to have any" I say in a whining voice.

"Well then when you are old enough I'll take you to have one" he says with a laugh.

That was enough embarrassment for one day for me, I skipped out of their room and into the kitchen. We had our breakfast and Victor offered me another ride on his motorcycle, it was too fun to say no to.

When we made it to the school I saw my new friend Niti in the parking lot, she saw who i was riding with and had the biggest smile on her face.

"So you and Victor?" she says the second we move away from the guys.

"He's my brother" I say in disbelief.

"Step brother" Niti reply saying the same words of my mother this morning.

"I can't fall in love with my step brother" I say trying to get away from the topic.

"Sure you can, at least he won't have to climb to your window at night" she says laughing

I look at her in disbelief before i break into laughter too, well she's right all he have to do is walk through the door.

7-Slipping

S ophia POV.

Niti made fun of me most of the day, she kept saying that Victor had the hots for me. I couldn't wait for us to have lunch, then I'll be sitting with the rest of them and she won't be able to say much.

My plan didn't really work since Victor sat next to me while she was facing me, she kept making kissy faces the whole time making me blush.

I also noticed Victor smile few times but he tried to keep it hidden.

"Hey little sis you want to see us play basketball?" Adam ask and I look at with confusion.

"There's a friendly basketball game today after class, you can stay and watch" he tell me.

"You play?" i ask him."All three of us do" Kyle reply instead. "Wanna come?" I ask Niti.

"And watch our school basketball team in all his glory? Well Duhh" she says and it's a deal.

Me and Niti spent the rest of the day together, Kyle finally giving us the freedom to walk to and from class alone.

After we finished the last period for the day we headed toward the stadium to watch the guys playing and clearly it wasn't just the two of us. Half of the school was there to watch, this is the first game of the year and everyone is here to cheer on the school team.

It was a bit too crowded, we searched for a place to sit and could hardly find any.

"Little sister" a voice said from behind me with hand coming around me.

I looked around to see Victor or maybe Adam standing behind me. I still had hard time knowing the difference. He was wearing a basketball Tshirt with tbe school logo on it and number twelve.

"Come sit here" he says guiding me and Niti to first raw seats, they said reserved on them but he just took the paper away and let me sit on it.

We had a front view of the whole game which was awesome, I still didn't know which one is Victor and which one is Adam. But they had the number twelve and six, Kyle was number eight.

I heard Sammy's voice from the other side of the gym, he was sitting with a group of his friends. He smiled and waved at me and i waved back.

When the game was over, the team that had twin number six won, although twin number twelve had Kyle with him.

"You wanna go down and say hi to the guys?" Niti ask me and I nod sure.

The second I got down Kyle asked for a hug since his team lost, making me giggle.

"Nu-uh you're full of sweat" I say taking steps back.

"Oh come here sister" he says chasing me, I went and hided behind twin number six.

"Let her go Kyle" he says."You're a fun killer Vic, really" Kyle replies.

Ohh, so it's Victor who won. He turn to me I smile and congratulates him.

"Thank you baby girl" Vic says giving me a slight hug.

"We're all going for lunch you wanna come?" Victor asks and I nod yes, I love spending time with them.

"Wait for me next to my bike, Niti can ride with the rest" He order and again I nod yes.

I was on the way out of the gym but there were just too many people, then I heard yelling and people started to push each other, I tried to take steps back but I was too late.

A guy from the team practically threw me back and I fell hitting my back and head hard.

I couldn't help but cry in that second, it hurt so much and my little side took control.

I felt strong arms come around my waist and picking me up, it was twin number twelve, Adam.

"You okay sis?" he asks, but I was too busy crying.

"Man she took a hit what should I do?" I heard Kyle voice.

"Go get Victor" Adam says trying to calm me down.

"Come on Soph, you're okay" I just hugged him and cried into his shoulder.

"Give her to me" I heard another voice, deeper voice, Victor.

He carried me and took me out of the gym, the cold air helped, but little soph was still out.

"You okay baby?" Victor asked, his voice wasn't helping my case.

"Huwt" I tell him pointing to my head.

"What happened there?" he ask, caressing my face.

"Too many peowple, fell" I tell him sniffling.

"I'm sorry baby" Victor tell me hugging me closer to his chest.

He was still a sweaty mess but he doesn't smell bad, he smell like musk and forest.

"Let's get you home baby" he says trying to set me down but I cling closer to him.

"Stay wid me" I say pleading with him.

"Yes baby I'll alway stay with you" his words were said in a way that made me feel he believed them.

He carried me back inside and took Adam's car keys and give him his motorcycle ones.

He opened the front door and set me in, he buckled my seat belt before going to the driver seat.

He turned the car in and drove us home, when we made it there he carried me again to my room.

"How about a nap?" he asks.

"Stay wid me" I demand again clinging to him even more.

He got in bed with me in his arms, he gave me my teddy Mr. Sparkle. I muzzled into his neck before falling asleep while breathing in his scent.

8-Avoiding.

I tried my best to avoid my step brothers, especially Victor, how embarrassing can it be.

I fell and acted like a total little and even clinged to him like a little girl wanting him to sleep next to me.

Ahhh, I felt so embarrassed, when I woke up I had my thumb in my mouth, please kill me now. He just smiled and told me I looked adorable.

The rest of the guys came in later, they all cooed at me. Even Alvin asked if I need him to kiss my boo-boo.

I refused polity only kicking his chin once, when dinner came I sat next to my mother trying my best to stay away from them.

I was excused with only eating half my plate and going to bed, I didn't say good night to any of them ans just ran and hide in my room.

I did that for the rest of the week, I even made mum or Niti drive me to school so I won't have to ride behind Victor, if they find out I'm a little they'll just make fun of me.

Kyle tried to talk to me in class but I just shushed him pretending to pay attention to the class and whatever it's about.

At lunch I made Niti sit with me away from my step brothers.

"Okay what's up soph? You've been avoiding them all week did something happen between you? Do I need to kick someone's ass?" she ask all serious.

"Nothing Niti" I lie through my teeth.

"Oh no don't you dare lying to me as your proclaimed best friend I need to know" she says and it's now or never.

"Victor saw me acting a bit weirdly" I say.

"Weird how girl?? He saw you sniffing through his underwear drawer?" she asks in all seriousness.

"What noooo!!!" I say quickly.

"Then whatever he saw you doing can't be that bad" she says shrugging.

I just nod and eat my food quietly, he saw me slipping, clinging to him, all I needed to do was call him daddy and die from embarrassment.

"Hey sis" Sammy says sliding next to me, I don't see him much during school since he's younger then me and spend most of his time with his friends.

"Hey Sammy" I say smiling, he's the cutest little bro ever.

"There's a game today us against the seniors. It's more like a friendly game would you stay and watch?" he ask and I think about, watching mean seeing all three of my brothers whom I'm trying to avoid, no thank you.

"Uhh no thanks Sammy I'll just head home" I say and his smile drop.

"Ohh, okay. I'll see you home then" he seemed to be really devastated that I won't be watching him play.

"Hey Sammy" I call him and he look back at me still with the sad smile.

"If you're playing then I'll stay to cheer you on" I say and it's like I got him a puppy for Christmas his smile was so wide it made me smile too.

"So your plan to avoid the hot step brothers came to an end?" Niti teases me.

I ignore her for now, only if she knew how weird I can be.

The rest of the day passed, Kyle didn't try talking to me anymore and I was grateful for that. It was all good until I had to go and watch Sammy play.

Again there were lots of people here to see and cheere for the younger team players. I was looking around for an empty place to sit when one of twins came and dragged me with him. He didn't have a shirt with his number on for me to know which one he is, I'm seriously having hard time with this. I should probably spend more time with them to know them apart, I was always bad with faces ans now it's bitting me in the bum.

He didn't make us sit in the front seet like last time, instead he drag us down to where the team is sitting. Sammy saw me and jumped toward me giving me a hug.

"You stayed" he says all happy."Of course I did" I say smiling back at him.

"Only the seniors are playing you can sit with the rest" the mysterious twin says.

I just nod, I sat and watched Sammy play he wasn't the best player but the seniors were more like professionals. They were taking it easy on them, passing the ball to them, it was just a friendly game.

"You know we kind of missed the good night's from you" the mystery twin says.

I just shrug again not knowing what to say, he get closer to me so we can have a half private talk.

"Why are you avoiding everyone?" he ask me again.

"Uhhh....it's just that...last time" I say and stop not sure what to say.

His eyes flashed for a minute and he got a sympathetic face on now.

"What did Victor do? He told me he just held you while you slept" he says, ahhh so he's Adam.

"I don't want him to think I'm weird" I mumble.

"Baby girl he'll never think you're weird, maybe he like weird too" he assure me.

"Not like it's just embarrassing" I say blushing.

"Nothing to be embarrassed off, I assure you that I...he...I mean all of us would never say anything to make you feel ashamed." he says again and I nod.

"But he's my brother" I whisper. "Step brother baby girl" he says with a wink.

Goddd what's wrong with all these people. Before I could say anything Sammy walked toward us, he just scored, well one of the seniors held him up so he can do a dunk, but a score none the less.

"Vic did you see me" he says to the twin sitting next to me, to Adam.

"I was like flying Vic, just like you" Sammy goes on.

I wasn't talking to Adam, god, how embarrassing can this be. I take off running outside of school.

9-Girls Talk.

I ran out but my ride was still there, I look around now what? I kept walking away from the school ground so Victor!won't be able to follow me.

I got my phone and called mum, she knows what to do she always do. When I slipped for the first time ever she knew what happened she talked to me about it and told me it's nothing to be ashamed of.

I'm not ashamed just embarrassed, my mom knowing and helping me is much different then my step-brother knowing and calling me about it.

Her phone rang and rang, I crossed my fingers that she'll reply but I was starting to lose hope and just before I closed the line she finally pick up.

"Hello" her voice came. "Mummy can you come get me" I say slipping to my younger self still embarrassed.

"I'll be there in ten" she replies.

Mum says people use this as a way to help with their stress and embarrassment, it's how it starts until you find how fun it is, even with just mum taking care of me.

I always acted younger then my age, I loved playing with barbies not being one like other girls in school. I knew I had to hide all this when mum got married, she deserves to be happy and I can be big, it's what I told myself before we came here.

I kept walking around just keeping an eye for my stepbrothers, they can't leave the game, and mum would be here soon. Ten minutes later she finally made it, I get in the car and just tell her to drive, rubbing my eyes feeling the pressure of a future headache.

"That bad Kido?" she asks me.

"Mummy...you don't even wanna know," I say with a sigh.

"Then I definitely want to know, this requires a girl night baby," she says.

We used to have girls' night all the time, just me and her, bad movies and tones of icecream, I know I could tell about anything, but I don't know if I'm ready to tell her about how I embarrassed my self in front of Victor. God why did I have to be so bad with faces, I swear I'm writing his name on his forehead so I'll never miss it again.

"What about Fred?" I ask, usually, at the end of our girl night, we'll fall asleep in the same bed.

"He can have a boy night or whatever they do, you'll have me all to yourself tonight" she says with a wink, just trust my mother to kick her husband out of bed and let me have a night with her.

"Fine mum but I want to watch Cinderella" she knows it's my favorite movie.

"Of course" she says with a knowing smile.

"And chocolate Ice cream" this time I say demanding.

"Nothing less for my favorite daughter" she replies with a smirk.

"I am your only daughter" I reply with a sigh, she always says the same, I wonder who's her favorite son now.

We did a quick turn to the grocery store getting ice cream, chips, and some other snacks. When we got home, I went to change my clothes to something more comfortable while she went to have a talk with Fred, probably giving a rundown of why he'll have to spend the night away from his own bed.

"Ready baby?" she asks dropping by my room, I had some sweats and the same shirt I slept in the first night I was here, I don't know who's the owner but I loved this shirt. We moved to her room and got Cinderella on. We ordered pizza for dinner and simply had some nice time, I kind of slipped to my little self, singing along the movie, getting food all over my face, just giggling over everything mummy said.

"Okay baby ready to tell me what's wrong?" she asks getting down to business.

I blush remembering the reason we're having this night, I slipped in front of my brother and then he lied to me, I really didn't like that one.

"Victor act like he Adam and made me tawk to him," I say with a big pout crossing my arms over my chest emphasizing how mad I am.

"Why would he do that Sophie?" she asks in a calm voice.

"Cause Vic saw me swipping and I was so embawassed and nu wanted to tawk" I tell her.

"Victor saw you slipping? That's why you've been avoiding the guys?" she ask and I nod, it's what I said.

"He acted all I Adam," I say really annoyed and on the verge of tears.

"He tricked you?" she say when I node she started to laugh, really laugh.

"Bad mummy" I say glaring at her, she's not supposed to laugh at me.

"Sorry baby, it's just he did the oldest twin trick and it worked," she says still laughing, okay maybe it is a bit funny.

"Okay baby I'm done laughing" she says gaining back her posture and giving me a real sympathetic smile.

"Look Sophia, your stepbrothers aren't that bad and I assure you they won't laugh or say anything that would make you feel bad. Maybe Victor like this too." she says making my cheeks glow red, is she really saying I should be with my brother.

"He's my brother!" I scoff.

"Stepbrother and I assure you I and Fred are okay with it," she says with a wink.

I felt my mouth fall open with shock, Ahhh, kill me now.

10-Frustrated.

V ictor POV.

     She won't talk to me, my wolf is going crazy, she won't look at me and now he feel like killing someone.

She doesn't want me or my brothers, her brothers now to drive her to school. Her mother would, or Niti who's a part of our pack, she's one hell of a smart wolf, strong dominant girl. I trust those too to keep her safe, I was very glad that she made friend with her on their first day.

They all know she's my mate, everyone but my mate knows, her avoiding me is going to be the death of me or one of my brothers.

They had their own theories of why she doesn't want to talk to us, she's avoiding everyone so something must have happened. Kyle, the smartass theory said when she hit her head it made her forget who we are and she needs another hit to remember. I forbids any more Tom&Jerry for that boy.

Alvin and Adam both said to just give her time, something my wolf can't take any more, he need to mark her, to make it known to everyone that she's mine. Sammy was only sad that his new sister wasn't really talking to him, well him and me both...

Kyle was the one keeping an eye on her during class, she's keeping close to Niti which is fine by me, as long as she's protected.

When the game came I couldn't take it anymore, and I wasn't about to let my mate sit in a random place, I brought her down so she can sit with us were I can make sure she's okay and she can actually see the others playing.

When I sat next to her I knew she wasn't sure if it's me or my twin, we look very similar but to any werewolf they knew me by my smell and aura. I'm their future alpha, my twin is strong but not as strong as me.

Since she didn't recognize her own mate yet I took advantage of it and asked her what's wrong. She kept saying about weird and embarrassment. I wanted to scream, I'm a daddy, I'm your perfect match and I'll kill anyone who dares make fun of you or our relation.

I was getting to my point without the screaming when Sammy came running and calling me my name. She took off running and my wolf was almost done with her, he wanted to catch her, mark her, and then tie her to his bed where no one can see her. We are possessive creatures, but I had better control and stayed in my seat, pure torture but better then scaring ten years out of my little princess.

Everyone's went home while I went on a speed ride on my bike, I needed the speed, the air hitting my face, I needed the relief. If I crash I won't die, I'll heal in few hours, a day max if I break too many bones.

I stayed outside for few hours, until it started raining and I had to go home, I don't mind getting wet but Anna, my new stepmother would kill me if I get the rugs filled with mud.

I came home and went in, my brothers were all in the entertainment room along with my father who was having a bear. There was no sign of the two female resident in the house.

"They are having a girls night" my father says making look at him all weird.

"She needs her mother for the night so I decided to spend my night with my boys" he says with a smirk, a night with the boys usually end up with us going wolf and ganging up on him.

"Ohh great Daddy you'll paint my nail and braid my hair?" Kyle asks making his voice extra high.

Everyone break to laughter, I even smile before turning to my father, I'm hurting and he'll knows what to do.

"Can I beat him now?" I ask, needing something to let the steam out.

"No you can't and Anna is talking with her, just give her a chance to get used to all this" my dad suggest.

"Why did she ran away from the game?" Adam asks.

Well now is the embarrassing part, we haven't do a you act as me stunt since we were six. Everyone can tell us apart, even with our matching tattoos, well except my new Sophia's one, it's right on my chest, that was a mother nature tattoo.

"I pretended to be you" I say getting ready for the worst.

They all break to laughter, Adam was on the ground laughing so badly, this wasn't really helping me or my moody wolf.

"Doesn't she know I'm the more handsome one?" Adam asks between laughter.

"Dad please, you don't need two of us. Can I kill him?" I ask again.

"Sorry Vic, I need both my boys" he replied making me groan.

If I can't kill any of my brothers, can't hold my little princess, I won't be staying here.

I left the house in a very bad mood, it was raining but I ignored it, I had to run a bit so I'm out of eye sight from the house before changing into my wolf.

Now on all four, I lift my head and let out a howl, filled with pain, I heard some of my packmates reply before I took off running.

I kept running until I found something I'm aloud to kill, a dear, it gave a little fight making me chase it around before I jumped and bites it in the neck. Killing it in just few minutes, my mouth was filled with blood, dinner is served but it wasn't near enough to help my wolf calm down.

11-Show Down.

S ophie POV.

After my girls night with mum I was feeling a little better, not much, I was still a bit confused. She doesn't mind me and Victor being together, isn't that just plain weird, the next morning I was kicked out of her room so Fred can come shower and change for the day.

I changed into some sweats and went down to the kitchen for breakfast, my brothers were there, all of them except Victor, they seemed to be tense. I said my good morning and took my seat next to Sammy, he tensed away once I sat I didn't understand why.

Alvin offered me a plate with pancakes with a kind smile before turning around and finish cooking. Mom and Fred came in next, we all ate breakfast with Victor missing, I just wanted to ask where is he? Is he okay?

But I kept my question to my self and sat quietly, once breakfast was over I decided to go out for a walk, getting some fresh air. I was just wandering around when I heard a strange sound, I looked behind me but saw nothing weird. I just kept walking not really caring when I heard a growl, a dog maybe, I looked around and saw a wolf.

I start to walk away slowly trying my best not to get the wolf's attention to me, the plan worked and I made it away, close to the house. I was almost there and ready to walk in when a very angry Victor came toward me, he looked furious.

"What are you doing out here?" he asks through gritted teeth.

"Uhh just walking around," I say feeling like a child getting scolded. His respond was a growl, a real growl at me, what's wrong with him.

"Didn't Alvin tell you not to get into the wood?" he asks through gritted teeth, I shrug well maybe he did I can't remember.

"How did they let you out alone" he asks again and I get enough with him, I'm not a child.

"I can walk around alone thank you very much" I say and try to turn around to leave but he doesn't let me go, he pinns me against the wall. His hands caging me, I shrunk on myself trying to get away.

Victor take a deep breath but then expire it next to my neck, I try to push him away, he's in my personal space but he won't budge.

"Victor get away" I say trying to push him with both my hands but it's like pushing a wall, it won't move.Instead he got even closer to me, his nose is in my neck now and I scream, he's scaring me.

He pull away and looks around searching for a danger, when he found nothing he turned back towards me. "Victor get away" I say and I'm sad to say, my voice did shake.

"NO" was his simple reply. Having enough of this I close my hand into a fist and try to punch him the face, in the movies they never show how hurt it does, or when the said person screams in agony.

"Fuck Sophia, are you okay?" Victor says while I scream, I think I broke my fingers.

He hold my hand with me crying and screaming, all this pain is sending me straight to my little space. He drags me crying and all inside the house, the others boys run toward the kitchen to see what's the commotion is about.

"She tried to punch me and hurt herself" Victor explains. Two minutes later my hand was wrapped with ice and I was still sobbing, only this time I'm cryint against Victor's chest.

"I'm sorry baby girl" he whispers while patting my head. "Next time you want to punch him just call one of us" Kyle says with a sarcasm.

I just give him a glare and ignore him, I finally stopped crying, my hand really hurt, Alvin checked it for me and said there's no breaking, still he wrapped it and gave me two Tylenol pills.

I was calm now, calm enough to notice Victor is the one holding me, that I'm practically sitting on his lap, I lose it again. I jump out and take few steps back.

"Stay away from me" I yell at him, he's back to growling at me, he's eyeing me with a dark look.

"Careful little girl" he warns me but I don't stop. "What's wrong with you!" I yell, my other four brothers still watching us.

"You can't avoid me Sophia" he says through gritted teeth, he looks like he's holding back, I don't really care.

"I can do whatever the Fuck I want" I yell back at him.

"You belong to me" he says in a whisper getting closer to me.

"Fuck you" I say and I lift my hand, to hit him again not learning my lesson, he catch it before it makes contact and that's when my mother come in the kitchen.

She looked at me with wild eyes, before her look turned to just mad, great.

"Sophia Marie Nightshade, what do you think you're doing" she scold using my full name.

"Mama it's....he's..." I try to explain things but she won't allow me.

"Save it! You don't try to hit anybody in this house, you don't curse!" she scolds and now I'm screwed.

"Consider yourself grounded, go to your room" she scold again and I run out of the kitchen, embarrassed, in pain, and crying.

12-Grounded.

Victor POV.

My wolf took control, he needed to touch her, to mark her as his. When I saw her in the woods I lost it, I shifted back just so I can yell at her, Alvin knows better than letting her out of the house, when I'm not around he should really keep an eye out since he's my second in commands.

Then my baby girl tried to punch me, if she didn't hurt herself I would probably punish her, it's not okay to hit me, not as her mate and future daddy nor as her alpha.

She tried to do it again and I stopped her, we don't have rules set yet, she doesn't really know much, but tell that to my possessive beast who just wants to make her call him daddy.

Before I could do or say anything that I'll regret later, her mother came in and she wasn't happy at all. She yelled at my baby and told her she's grounded, my poor baby she left crying and her face a new shade of red.

Once she got claimed by wolf rules, any kind of discipline would be made by her mate, that would be me. Since we weren't official yet it was still up to her mother, who's giving me a questioning look right now.

"She shouldn't go into the woods, not alone. The rest was just a little tantrum" I say explaining things to her.

She nods her then sigh, we had a talk about her daughter being my mate, she's mated to my father and knows how possessive us wolves can be.

"She's mad because you saw her slipping then you did that Adam stunt, I tried explaining things to her, assured her that I'm okay with it," she explained.

Gahh, I knew I shouldn't have done that, but I couldn't not talk to her, I just needed my chance. Leaving the little girl to calm down, I stayed out of her hair and her room until later, when I was risking my wolf going out again and going to find her. I made her some cookies, I knew she liked chocolate from her staying with us, so chocolate cookies it was.

When the cookies were still warm I placed them on a plate along with a cup of milk I went to her room, I knocked, and waited for her to answer. It took her a minute but a puffy-eyed Sophia opened the door for me, she had clearly cried, my heart broke, knowing I'm the reason for her tears.

"I got you cookies," I say lifting the plate showing her my peace offering.

She frowns and pouts, she was about to close the door in my face, I place my foot against the door not allowing it to close. She looks at me with a glare on her pretty face, she's ready to hit me again, I'm sure.

"Come on pretty girl, who says no to chocolate cookies?" I say again and a look pass on her face, no little would say no to cookies, none that I heard off.

She opens the door for me to come in, she went and sat on her messy bed trying to hide the teddy bear. I smile at her trials, I set the cookies and milk on her bedside and sit next to her on the bed.

"What's his name?" I ask pointing to the bear that she's practically sitting on right now, I need her to know that I'll never make fun of her. Her face turns red and she shakes her, not willing to share. I lift her up and get the teddy from underneath her.

"Come on a pretty teddy like this one deserves a name," I say encouraging her.

"Mr. Sparkle" she mumbles her face ten shade redder.

"What a great name" I reply with a big smile, she steals few glances up my face making sure I'm not fooling her. My smile gets wider and she actually smiles back for once, wanting to end her misery I just get straight to the point.

"I'm sorry for pretending to be Adam, but you wouldn't talk to any of us. It's okay if you're a little we'll never judge you. Wanna know a secret" I whisper in her ear and she nods.

"I'm actually a daddy," I say and she just gasps, her mouth falling with how shocked she is.

"You...you...." she stutters.

"Yes I and everyone in the house knows, we don't hide things from each other okay. It's okay to be you" I assure her again and she nods with a big blush.

"Now cookies?" I ask.

"Cookkkkiiieees" she says with a big nod. I gave her the plate along with the milk glass, she really enjoyed them.

"You know baby girl, if you promise not to hit or yell again I can talk to your mother about being grounded," I say causally wiping off her milk mustache.

"Really?" she asks with a raised brow.

"Yes really, if you let me take you out on a date" I add, I really want to get to know my baby girl, if she knew who I am, if she knew what she is to me. We wouldn't need any date for her to know she's my everything, she blushes at the request and thinks about it for a bit before nodding her head.

"We got a deal," I ask.

"Deal" she whispers back.

13-Date.

Sophia POV.

I had a date with my step-brother, I had a date with my step-brother, ahhhh...I changed my clothes a hundred times not knowing what to wear. I can't google what to wear for my date with my step-brother. Ahh...mom is gonna help, should I go with something girly or something more big girls like.

"I think this will do" my mother held up a baby blue dress, it stop at mid thighs and got long sleeve. The weather is getting colder and this would be perfect, I took the dress and put it on along with some black tights.

For shoes I had on my converse on, I'm not good with heels. My mom helped with my white hair, and make up, I didn't know where we are going but she said I'm dressed perfectly.

Victor talked her into ungrouding me, he even talked her into letting me go out with him. How many girls can say hey mom, I'm going out with my step brother.

I walked downstairs to see all my step-brothers waiting downstairs not just Victor. Alvin did low cat call whistle while Adam gave Vic a slap on the back with good luck.

Kyle was on my side alone with Sammy, I got a kiss from each tellimg me to tell them in case Victor does anything, they were playing the role of overprotective brothers making me giggle.

Victor took me to Adam's car instead of the motorcycle, he opened my door for me, helped me sit, strapped me in and closed the door before getting in.He still refused to tell me how he convinced my mother into letting us go or where we are going, no matter how much I asked or whined on the way there.

I'm still new to this town, but from where we are going, I know we are heading outside, but where exactly.Victor just smiled and teased me with the word "you'll see" the whole way until we drove for about an hour.

When Victor parked the car I could see fairy lights, smell sugar and grease in the air. We are at an amusement park, I haven't been in one in forever, I squealed with happiness the little side of me taking over. I tried to rain it in, not wanting to show Victor little Sophie with all her glory.

"Anna helped choosing the place, she said you'd like it here" Vic says, of course my mother helped. "I love it" I say not able to hide my excitement and he smile at me."Shall we?" he says once he opened my door and took the seatbelt off.

We walk in and buy our tickets, I wanted to play with everything. Forgetting my decision about raining it in, I drag Victor with me to the rides. We start with cars, classic, we stood in line with me jumping up and down the whole time. Other people eyed me but one glare from Victor had them looking the other way, he held my hand through the line but when the time for driving came I beated his ass.

I laughed badly when he got stuck in the corner with others hitting him. When the ride was over Victor held my hand and took me toward the next ride. We went through them all, the rollercoaster, the carousel horses, the cars, and finally the ferries wheel.

When the wheel stopped with us on the top, he squeezed my hand a little getting my whole attention, he landed a sweet kiss on my hand smiling.

"If you'd let me I would love to be your caregiver" he says making me look at him with wide eyes he just smiled and went back to enjoying the ride.

After our last ride we decided it was enough with the rides and just held hand while walking around. I got some cotton candy that we shared, I never went on a date or enjoyed it like this one. It was perfect.

Victor wanted to play a game of throw the ball and hit the bottles before we left, he got them down on his first trial. He chose a big white teddy and gave it to her, this date couldn't get any better.

They got in the car and drove back to their town, not before stopping for MacDonald, she had the happy meals while he had two big mac, god,can he eat.

The rest of the drive was filled with laugh and giggles I didn't know Victor can be so funny. We did talk a bit about everything, from the town to his siblings, how I felt about having four new brothers, they are my brothers but not him, he's something else now.

When we got home I was tired, he helped me and the teddy out of the car and into the house, everyone was eyeing us to see how our date went making me blush and Victor sneer at them. He walked me up to my room, were we stood nose to nose, he leaned closer and closer until our lips met in the middle, my first kiss.

"Think about it, baby girl" he whispered in my ear before leaving.

How did the day change from me punching him to him kissing me.

(A thank you to my friend for help with this idea. She got a story going on, check her out jf you want)

14-Daddy.

Victor POV.

My wolf was finally at peace, he took our mate on a date and even asked her to be her daddy, she didn't agree nor disagreed yet but that's a start, all he has to do is wait for her reply. She says yes in the end, even if she's just a quarter breed the wolf blood in her would make her feel a pull toward me too.

I went to sleep with a happy smile on my face, all I needed right now was Sophia to be in my arms and I'll die a happy man, my wolf agrees, he wants our mate too. Her smell was still stuck on me which helped my possessive beast until she could decides if she wants to be mine or if she wants to be mine.

There's no other options, not for me at least, she's my everything. This night felt extremely long, the morning just refused to come out for me to find out her answer. I thought about going for a run but what if she needed me during the night. Plus I need to be here first thing in the morning when she wakes up to tell me she agrees, she gotta agree, we're mate for heavens sake, I was made for her.

After turning for the millionth time in bed, the day light was finally starting to show, I looked at my clock to see it's five thirty am, almost time for the princess to wake up.

I'm just praying that she won't sleep in tonight when I heard the tiniest knock on my door, followed by my door being open slighty. And in came my princess in all her glory, she had her teddy in her hand, dressed in baby blue pyjamas, her hair was wild but she looked beautiful.

"Everything okay princess?" I ask her worried. "I couldn't sleep" she begins and I sit stright in my bed patting a spot next to me.She ran toward me and took a seat next to me, her head went over my shoulder.

"Something in me kept nagging at me to come here. Now that I'm here, it's weird Vic, it's like something insides me just want to stay close" she says her eyes close and her nose getting closer to my neck, she doesn't understand what's happening but a part of her, a certain wolf part of her is marking their territory over me.

I let her nuzzle into my neck until she's satisfied, her eyes flew open and she blush, what just happened wasn't really a conscious move. I just smile showing her It's okay, that she can show me all parts of her and I'll still take her anytime.

"I couldn't sleep either just thinking if you'll be mine or if you'll be mine" I tell her and she chuckles.

"Isn't supposed a no or yes answer?" she says in a sassy voice. "I'm hoping for the latter" I say nuzzling her neck now, it was my turn to mark her.

I'll explain everything about being mates later, I just don't want to overwhelm her right away. Everything will make sense once she knows what we are for each other.

"I want to be yours" she whisper. "I was hoping you'd say so" I say unable to hold my self or my happiness I trap her on my bed between my arms and openly nuzzle her neck making her giggle.

"Sophia Marie Nightshade would you do me the honour and be my little girl?" I ask her officially again. "Yes Victor I would" she replies with red cheeks. "Ohh no that's daddy for you little misses" I say fake biting her neck making her giggle even louder.

I was now the happiest werewolf to ever exist, the sound of my mate laugh was priceless to me, it made me smile involuntary. After her last giggling fit Sophia let out a loud yawn, I guess we should catch some Zzz.

"Come on little one let's sleep a little" I say sliding her and me under the covers, I save her teddy from the floor and hand it over to her. We both fall asleep hugging each others like we're supposed to.

I woke up to some giggling sound between my arms, I know those giggles, I hug her tighter.

"I think she can't breath" I hear my youngest brother voice now."Maybe we should save her from the beast. Blink twice if you need help" that of course was Kyle voice.

What are they doing in my room, I groan but keep my eyes closed hoping they'll go away.

"Ohh look how adorbale they look but do you think she can breath" my twin voice join them, is there a meeting in my room that I didn't know about.

Another giggle from the little one in my arms before she tries to get up, I try to pull her back down.

"Ignore them and they'll leave" I say to her. "Really man? We're here to say congratulations" Alvin our oldest was here too!

This time I do open ny eyes and sit up, all of my siblings were in my room watching me and the little sleeping, we are a close family but this is too much.

"Creepy much guys?" I ask them. "Anna told us the good news" Kyle says and I look at him with confused look how did she know. I turn back to my littl who was now blushing.

"I needed her opinion" she says casually. "Yup at 2 o'clock in the morning" Adam adds with a laugh making the little one blush even more.

I guess our sleeping time is over, I have to hear this story.

(Every time u see an update just know I can't sleep . It's 2:30 am for me. Hope u enjoy, and please vote and comment for me)

15-Fussy.

S ophia POV.

I couldn't sleep, I just couldn't just thinking about Victor next door, after our date he asked to be my daddy and that I should just think about it. Well I've been thinking about it most of the night, I decided to go ask mom for help, she's my parent for a reason and she has to help me even if it's two am in the morning.

I left my bed and went to hers and Fredrick's room, I knocked first not ready to see my step dead naked, I waited for a minute then knocked again. This time Fred opened the door for me, he looked at me with surprise before asking what's wrong.

"Are you okay Soph?" he asks.

"Can I come in?" I ask him, needing to talk with my mother.

He invites me in, I go to their bed and shake my mother awake, she looked at me with a confused look before turning to her husband who just went back to bed.

"Can't it wait for the morning Sophia?" she asks, she knows I'm here for something and I'm not in my little space, if I was scared I'll run in crying and calling for her.

"No it can't I need help now," I tell her honestly and she sits up in bed to hear what I got.

"Victor asked me to be my daddy," I tell her.

"That's great news honey, and it can definitely wait till the morning," she says before going back to bed.

"Nuu mum stay up, I don't know if I should say yes or no," I say this is something very important she can't just ignore me.

"I think you two were made for each other Sophia and your mother agrees. You got our blessing baby girl, now go annoy my son so we can sleep" Fred says, I kind of forgot he was there with us too.

"What he said Soph now out" my mother kicked me out, well thanks to a lot mother!

I went back to my room and kept thinking about it until I could master enough courage to go talk to Victor, so what if the hour was almost six am. That was one of my best decisions ever, we ended up falling asleep together in his bed, I only woke up to see all our siblings in his room looking at us.

Mum told them about our little rendezvous, at two am, that traitor. We got out of bed, I went to my room to get ready before we both went down for breakfast. We had waffles with ice cream and strawberries for breakfast, everyone was celebrating us for becoming a couple.

Kyle and Adam took celebrating and teasing me way too far, they decided to just call me baby for the rest of the day, and baby me the whole day. It was fun first but then they started to get on my nerves, when they asked if I need to go potty or they need to hold my hand on the stair for the tenth time I decided to get my revenge and hit Adam with a good fist on his shoulder.

"Hey what's that for?" he asks in disbelief, so I punched him again.

"No need for violence little sis or I'll call Vic" Adam threatens.

"Call him!" I say having enough with him, before leaving him and moving down the stairs, Alvin was my only ally today since he didn't try to baby me or tease me for being with Victor now.

Me and Alvin played video games, I wasn't that good at it but he still let me won few times making me jump up and in happiness before I went in for a hug.

I felt strong hands on my waist pulling me back toward a strong chest, then I felt a warm breath at my neck and a growl, did Victor just growls. I turn to him but his eyes were fixed on Alvin who's now looking down to the floor.

Victor pulls me into his lap, I didn't want to play anymore, I just sat there with him, even with his strange feeling I felt safe around him. Speaking of safe I need to call Niti or she'll have my head monday for keeping it away from her.

I try to get up from his lap but he won't let me, I try again and Victors arms get even tighter.

"Vic let me go" I say but he doesn't."No" he replies."Victor please" I say honestly trying to fight his hands off me, but he wouldn't let go.

"Ahhh, Alvin help" I turn to him for help, he turns to Victor and speeks slowly keeping his eyes low.

"Victor, you need to let Sophia get up, you're hurting her" he says very slowly like he's speaking to a wild animal, it felt like it with how hard he's holding to me."Victor, you're hurting Sophia now let her go" this seems to do the trick and he let me go.

The second I felt his hands losen around my waist I get up and move away, he had a big pout on his face after I moved. I still ignored it and run to my room to call Niti, she picked up right away and screamed in my ear when I told her about, well about everything.

I ended my call with Niti and stayed in my room until dinner time, I didn't sit next to Vic, I sat next to Sammy which made Vic growl, he stood next to Sammy and the poor guy just fell off the chair trying to move fast enough.

He took Sammy's place next to me, he fussed over me and my food, cutting my food to smaller bite size and feeding me. It felt nice to be spoiled by Vic but every time I even moved an inch from him he's pout and fuss until I was close to him again.

By bed time Victor begged me to sleep in his room with him, for the first time ever I felt like I'm the one dealing with a fussy little and not the other way round, what's up with Victor.

(It's Saturday It's My Bday!!! Heheheh I'm 25 now, did you like the chap? How about a fussy daddy for once, ohh and it's not even 2am(it's 1:52))

16-Secret.

V ictor POV.

"Can you stop being fussy" Alvin asks, it's the morning, Sophia left my bed this morning before I woke up.

I found her taking a shower and getting ready for school, I fussed over her wet hair making sure to dry it and style it for her, we might be an all guys house but I still learned how to do hair with the rest of the pack, I knew I'll have to know to style my future baby hair.

"I'm not fussy" I snap at my brother, she kicked me out of her room to get dressed while I sat down in the kitchen still in my pajamas.

"Really you're fussy every time Soph even leave your sight, last night you scared Sammy so much he slept in my bed" Alvin says with a sigh.

Sammy our youngest wasn't the most dominant in our home, he's a bit sensitive too. Me snapping at him last night maybe wasn't my best move, I just had to sit next to my mate, I wanted to mark my mate.

This whole crazy pull would calm down after she accept me as her mate. We don't have to do anything, she just need to accept me as hers, I already accepted her the second I saw her.

"Go get dressed man, maybe we should tell her and be over with it" my brother and beta says.

We're brothers, he's older then me, he's my beta, he gets a free pass most of the time. With a sigh I made it to my room and got dressed, I walked back down to see Sophia hugging Sammy, I don't think when I pull her toward me, my face burried in her neck.

"Daddy what's wrong with you" my baby snaps at me, she called me daddy, dear god she called me daddy.

I think my eyes just did the heart emoji shape, I couldn't help but smile, she can snap and yell for all I care she just called me daddy.

"He's a lost cause little sis" I hear Kyle says as Alvin hugs a now sobbing Sammy, I'm his alpha, me snapping and scaring him twice in such a short time isn't helping my case.

I snap out of it and try to talk to my brother who just cowers away from me, my mate she looks so mad, she turns to Adam my twin.

"I'm riding with you guys" she says and they nod."You coming Sammy or you gonna spend the day in Alvin lap" Kyle teases.

Sammy lift his head from Alvin lap and leave with the rest not sparing me a second glance, I'll have to work this one soon. My mate leave with my brothers and before I had the chance to run after her Alvin holds me back.

"You need to stop being fussy and tell Sophia" Alvin says. "You want me to do a twilight scene and tell her our ancestors story over a bonfire" I ask with fake enthusiasm.

"We don't have a story you idiot, the goddess created us and what ours" Alvin says in disbelief not getting the joke.

"I know you moron, I just go and say hey baby I'm a werewolf and so are you?" I ask. "Practically she's only quarter wolf and no! Make it romantic" my brother says.

Make it romantic my ass, I get my bike keys and leave after them, if I'm lucky I'll get there before the bell and get to see Sophia before her classes. Sadly even with breaking speed I made it late to class, Soph was already in hers.

Kyle messaged me saying he'll walk her to classes while I thought about ways to tell her our secret, I can't wait much longer, her simply accepting to be my baby girl wasn't enough.

I'm a beast in the inside, I needed to know she accept me before I went crazy with need. I wasn't paying attention to any of my classes, until an idea came to me, just the way to tell Sophia and one that isn't taken from twiligh movie.

I messaged Kyle and Adam telling them to keep an eye on her while I got my surprise ready, a way to show her how much she means to me and my wolf.

I also asked them to drive her over once the school was over, I can try to be a romantic guy but this is the best I could come up with.

After school, Adam drove avery confused Sophia to the middle of the woods under a giant oak tree, a picnic was waiting for her.

"Good luck sis" Adam said before leaving a very confused Sophia with me.

"Sophia" I say, my whole body tense, what if she refused me.

"A picnic" she asks in a confused voice and I take her hand and show her to the already there blanket spread on the ground. We both sit down and I couldn't help but tell her everything.

"Under an oak tree, thousands of years ago a goddess sat, they say she's the goddess of the moon. She loved the earth, her favorite place was one similar to this, whenever she came and sat down here a wolf would come to her. She loved the wolf, they became friends the legend says they could understand each others" I start and see I have Sophia full attention.

"When the wolf got too old and died, the goddess missed him, in honor of their friendship she created a new race, a mix of humans and her old friend, she didn't made them alone to every wolf there was a soul mate, one that they would die to protect" I continue and she nods her head.

"I'm one of the moon goddess creation Sophia so are you, well quarter of you" I say with a nervous smile.

"What? What are you talking about?" Sophia asks in confusion.

"It's just best I show you" I say and get to my feet, I close my eyes and let my wolf side takeover. Once I'm standing on four feet I saw Sophia eyes goes wide before she whispers. "Beautiful"

(Thank you for all the Bday wishes. Ps:I love twilight, do u like this wolf legend or should I eddit it? It's only 12:40am I'm early today)

17-Quarter.

Sophia POV.

Victor been acting weird all day, the way he talked to Sammy this morning, he made him cry, I was so mad at him for that.

Alvin explained things to me saying Sammy is a special boy, I didn't know if that means he's a little or not but I still loved my brother. Victor acting like an ass wasn't helping, I was mad and ended up riding with Sammy, Kyle and Adam to school.

I didn't see Victor at lunch break, Adam said he's busy but he's here to keep me company. I slapped his shoulder at that. Sammy sat with us instead of his friends, he gave me a sad smile and that was it from Sam, I hardly ate anything and that was just due to Niti and Kyle encouragement.

The rest of the day passed with me thinking where the hell Victor is, it wasn't until the school day ended and instead of all of us going home, Alvin picked the rest while Adam said he's going to drive me to Victor.

"He's just being fussy because he want to tell you something" Adam says, if this is his trial of making me feel better, well it didn't work, now I'm even more nervous.

Adam dropped me in the middle of the wood, is this the point where he kills me and get rid of the body, Victor guides me to under a giant tree, he has a picnic all set for us, and I doubted my daddy.

It's still hard to think about him as my daddy, I never had one before, this is all so new to me, when he started telling me the story, I felt so related to it, I could just imagine myself under the tree, seeing the wolf, it all felt so real.

Then he said it's real, he's one of them, I felt my heart miss few beats, when the wolf stood in front of me instead Victor, he had the same green eyes as Victor, brown coat like my daddy's hair. He was simply, Beautiful, did I just said that out loud.

I saw the wolf smirk at me, could wolf even do that, he got closer to me and took a deep breath, smelling me, he then used his nose to nuzzle my neck, this wasn't any normal wolf, he was huge, and with me being short, we stood on some eye level.

After he was done with my neck he took a step back and Victor stood instead of the wolf, his clothes still there, I guess the clothes going away is just a myth.

"Are scared baby girl?" Victor asks one hand going up my face to caressing it.

I mean into his touch and shake my head no, I wasn't scared, I felt safe with him. He smiled at that, a big smile showing off his beautiful smile.

"Do you still want me to be your daddy?" he asks next and I still nod.

"Sophia do you know what you are for me?" he asks and I shakemy head no.This time he does take his shirt off, I guess there's some stripping after all, once his shirt was off, showing off a tanned body with tattoo covering most of his hands and shoulder, but the one that got my full attention is my name in full black ink right on top of his heart.

"This one" he says pointing to my name. "It wasn't made by a needle, this one was made by the goddess, the moon goddess decided to gift all the wolf ascendant with mates, your name was carved on my chest the second I saw you sleeping in that car, I knew you were mine" he says making my mouth fall open.

"I...I..." I stutter."You only have to accept me as yours Sophia, if you do my wolf and your wolf side would be connected for life" he says.

"I don't have a wolf side" I say, if I turned to a wolf or was a descendant from the moon goddess I would've known.

"You are baby, you are quarter wolf" he replied with a smirk.

"How?" I ask in disbelief."Your mother is a half breed, her mother before her was a full wolf" he explain.

I never knew my grandma, mother grew up with her father only, this mean I'm a quarter a wolf.

"Can I?" I ask excited can I change too?"No baby you can't I'm sorry, but you may be able to hear your wolf side" he adds.

"I got a wolf side?" I ask again. "Yes you'll be able to hear her, she won't be able to shift but she'll still want to play with her mate" he explains to me.

"Do I get a tattoo too?" I ask."No only the more dominant get the tattoo" he says with a smirk.

"What does that means?" I ask.Victor had me pinned against the tree trunk with both my hands above my head while he whispered in my ear.

"That means only daddies and mommies get tatoo, pretty little girls like you don't, I'm sorry baby" he explains to me making me smile and maybe slip a little.

"Me pway with wolfie?" I ask, I already named his wolf side, well for me I did.He just look me and shake his head with a smile, before turning back to his wolf form and letting me play with him.

(12:07 am, sorry people I've been sick a little. My sick brain wanna do a part two with Sammy and a mommy, do u think I should do it? it would be an individual story of course)

18-Questions.

After I slipped to my little space there was no coming back, I was just my little self then. I played with daddy in his wolfie form, I jumped on his back playing fight while he gently let me down again.

He loved nuzzling my neck, I also found out that pulling his tail was a big no-no since he growled at me when I did that. We played for about an hour or so until I got too exhausted to play anymore, it's when he said it's time to leave.

We got out picnic all packed up and ready to go, we left in a car instead of his motorcycle, he told me it's his but he doesn't like to drive it around, a bike is much easier.

I fell asleep on the ride back home, I didn't feel a thing when daddy Victor carried me upstairs or when he tucked me in bed taking my shoes off. He even gave me my teddy Mr. Sparkle, when I woke up after my nap it was in his bed and not mine, he was sitting right next to me looking at me, it was creepy and sweet in the same time.

"Good morning sweet girl" he says once he saw I'm awake."Had a nice nap?" he asks ans I nod. "Sophia can you be big for me for a minute?" he asks and I nod.

I sat up in bed and focused on being big, it was a bit hard but I did it, he smiled at me before he started talking.

"I don't want to force you to answer me Sophia, but I need to know my wolf need an answer. Do you accept us as your mate?" he asks.

He did tell me the goddess made us for each others, I'm his mate but now I didn't know what to say, a part in me said yes while another part of me was scared.

"Are mate like soulmate?" I ask."Yes it's exactly the same, you are everything your mate need you to be, we can never hurt our soulmate and would never let anyone hurt them" he explains.

"And what if I'm scared?" I ask. "I know baby, I'm sorry that I'm forcing you to make a decision this fast, but when we find our mate we go crazy until they accept us. I'm sorry I shouldn't force you, you can think about it first okay?" he assures me with a smile.

We moved out of the bed next, he told me to go do my homework, mate or not I'm still his little girl. I moved to Kyle's room under the pretentious of doing homework together, Kyle's room was a messy room, it was filled with posters and pictures all over, it was filled with life just like my brother.

We did our homework together which ended up being Kyle copying mine, afterward I had to ask him about the whole mate thing.

"Ahh I see, well like Vic said when you find your mate you go crazy until they accept you" he says. "What does accepting means?" I ask.

"It's just you saying the words I accept you as mine and me as yours" he says with a smirk, I knew Kyle enough now to know there's more to it, I raise a brow and wait.

"Well just words that tie up your two wolf form, you'll be able to communicate telepathically, your bond will form, his possessive beast will finally rest cause you'll smell like your dominant" he explains.

"Whut?" I ask with an open mouth making Kyle fall off his chair in a laughing fit, he must be messing with me.

"Hey I'm serious! Just ask your mother" he says offended, my mother?

"My mama?" I ask again feeling slow today. "Your mother is my father mate Sophia, it's obvious" he says making me feel extra dumb now.

The quick wedding, moving to the other part of state with Frederic, of course they are mates and here I am wasting my time with Kyle.

I ran toward my mother who's in the kitchen busy doing dinner with my step dad.

"Hey dad you mind if I steal mom. Thanks love you" I say dragging my mother from her hand along with me.

"What's up with you?" mom ask once we're in my room. "I know about the wolf thing, I know about the mating but I don't know what to say to Victor" I say in a hurry.

"He told you?" she asks and I nod yes, it's what I said. "Well you can say yes and you two would start to bond baby, the bond won't be completed until you two do the deed which I don't expect my girl to do anytime soon" she says in her mother voice and I just nod.

"The bond baby is kind of scary but believe me no one would love you like your mate would, my father always told me about the love he shared with mom. He was a human but he was her mate, it's a rare thing for someone with no wolf in him to have a human mate. Even after she left us he still remembered their time together and how much they loved each other" mom says with a sad voice, okay maybe being bonded isn't that bad.

"You won't believe me until you try it Sophia, trust your mother on this one baby girl" she ends with a wink.

I think I'm going to trsut my mother as she said, before I could say anything else she adds.

"And you just called Fred dad, he's been jumping and screaming in my head, he's hooked now baby, you'll have to keep doing it" she said with a wink. I did call him dad didn't I.

After spending ten full minutes of thinking I decided to just let nature take it's course, I ran toward Victor.

"I accept you as mine and me as yours" I say and he breaks into the biggest smile ever before engulfing me in a bear hug.

(1:06am, to the people who said yes on the Sammy story, do it now? Or wait till this one is over?)

19-Accepted.

V ictor POV.

She just accepted me as hers, she said the words, the sun brightened, the moon got it's shine back, the world went back to normal. My baby just accepted me as hers, I'm now her daddy and mate, I couldn't be happier or prouder of myself.

I engulfed her in a bear hug, crushing her close to me, marking her as mine, with her now accepting, her wolf side accepting mine, we smell the same, like mates. She have a lot of me on her, the more dominant always get to scent and mark his little one.

"I love you Sophia, I love you so much. You make me the happiest person on planet earth" I tell her, she might not believe me, but for me I adore her.

"Something in me screams I love you back but I don't really know" she mumbles, she doesn't get it yet but it's okay.

"It's okay baby you don't have to say it back" I tell her, I can say it for both of us, I can scream it from top of the roof about how much I love her.

She just smiles at me, that adorable smile of hers, making my heart melt, wanting to show off more about our mating bond I close my eyes and speak but not loudly, I use our bond to talk to her.

"I love you little one" I say and she jumps up with big wide eyes, she start to look around and then at me.

"It's the way mates can communicate, you could be in the end of the world and I'll be able to reach you" I explain to her.

"Can I try?" she asks and I nod in encouragement. She closes her eyes and try her best to send me a message, it was a bit mixed up and she mumbled in the same time.

"Did it work?" she ask me with wide doe eyes."Yes but you only have to think about it no need to say it out loud" I explain to her and she nods yes.

"Come on let's go tell everyone" I say and drag her with me toward the living room, my brothers knew about it they saw how anxious I was waiting for her reply.

I found them in the entertainment room, even my father and step mother were there.

"She accepted" I say loudly, everyone got up and congratulate us. No one dared to hug Sophia, she's mine, my wolf only allowed Sammy to give her a quick hug, along with our parents.

After telling the family the good news, we went back up to our bedrooms, I asked Sophia to move in to mine, it's nothing sexual, I just crave to stay close to her and it'll give me a better chance of taking care of her and her little side.

We spent the afternoon moving her stuff to my room, the day have passed, it was a very long day indeed. By diner time my little one was exhausted, she could hardly eat with how sleepy and tired she was. Me being a good daddy and mate, I picked her into my lap and fed her most of her plate, we said our goodnight and moved to bed, I brushed her teeth for her and gave her the same Tshirt she slept in the first night.

We moved to bed and I was just a happy man, Sophia's head was burried in my neck, even in her sleep she was nuzzling me. It was a miracle that I could sleep that night with how excited about everything I was, but eventually I did.

We had school the next day, I woke up and went to get ready giving my princess a little more time to sleep. After getting ready I went toward her and tried to shake her awake, landing few kisses on her face, petting her hair, she woke up opening only one eye at before seeing it's me and smiling.

"Come on little one it's time for school" I tell her and help her getting ready for the day. We moved for breakfast where my brothers thought now it's safe for them to make jokes about me.

"Ohh look at the love birds" Alvin starts. "Really sis you could've at least chose me, I'm the better looking one" Adam my twin tease."Just look at the heart eyes in his cold stoned face" Kyle adds with a smirk.

I ignored them long enough for me to make sure Sophie is sitting and have a plate in front of her before I went for their necks. Sammy who was sitting next my baby watching the whole thing and laughing, she looked at me, then the rest of the family and joined in the laughing fit, my brothers joined too, you'd think we're a pack of hyenas not wolves.

"Eat your breakfast little one" I say and go back to sit, she still chuckled but ate her food.

After breakfast she got on the motorcycle behind me for the ride to school. I helped her down and took the helmet off her head, we walked in the school holding hands, it's when Niti my baby friend saw us, well she smelled us.

"Oh My God!" she said out loud, she's a wolf, all the pack would know by the end of the day that Sophia accepted me, all hail the new Luna.

(12:52am, about the Sammy story, I started that one, do u want to see it now with slow updates or after I finish this one? Also do u have any suggestion for me? Don't forget to vote. Message me sometimes, I get bored)

20-Luna.

"Oh My God!" was Niti's first comment when she saw me, did she knew? How did she know what happened, maybe she's just saying so because she saw me get off Vic's bike.

She just nodded toward Vic before dragging me with her in the school away from my stepbrothers and into a more isolated place. I could hear daddy's chuckle in my head, this whole telepathy is still weird for me.

"You and Victor? Finally?" she asks.

"How did you know?" I ask the obvious question.

"You smell like him" she replies like it's nothing and I look at her with confusion, wait how could she smell Vic on me?

"He didn't tell you? Really?" she asks offended. I look at her but still don't get it, so I decided to ask daddy about it. I try my best to think about him and send him a message,

"Is Niti?" was all I had to say before he replies. "Yes she's a wolf baby girl" was his reply, now my mouth does fell open with shock, and she didn't tell me! And he didn't tell me! Those two traitors!

"Tell me all about it1 Did you do the?" she ask with a wink.

"Niti!!" I say in a squeaky voice, she just says what and laughs.

"How did you know?" I ask her again.

"You smell like the alpha, well you smell of alpha and just a little bit of you," she says.

"What alpha?" I ask again.

"The alpha, Victor, your mate" she explains.

"Daddy," I ask through our bond. "Yes, baby girl?" he replies. "Are you the alpha?" I ask not really believing. "Yes I am" he replies like it's nothing.

"Did you ask him?" she says with a smirk. How does she know so much!

"No fair Niti! How do you know so much?" I say in a pouty voice.

"You're just adorable, I bet you're a little too and hiding it from me," she says in accusation.

"NITI! How!" I yell, okay she won, how does she know this much about me!

"Alpha Vic is a daddy, you showed some little behaviors, I'm not stupid you know" she says and I nod she's not stupid at all.

"Come on you can tell me all about it after school," she says and I nod yes, we need to sit down and talk for sure.

All during class and school hours every time I passed by people's heads would turn toward me, some would look at me with big wide eyes, others would just nod for me while I passed. Kyle and Niti were having too much fun over my back when they asked to be forgiven over the missed homework, saying they were busy with me. Then at PE Niti said we can't play, the teacher took one look at me and nodded his head yes letting us sit on the bench while the others had to run laps.

When lunchtime came, I ran toward Vic, all this extreme attention was getting the best of me, I couldn't take anymore from this. He pulled me into his hands and just growled, it was a low voice but I could hear it, feel his chest rumbling, everyone looked the other way now, no one was sparing us a look finally I could breathe.

"You okay baby?" daddy asks and I just nod my head, I was feeling too overwhelmed right now but trying my best not to slip to my little self.

The rest of the day passed a bit better now, no one was looking at me the same way and Vic told Kyle off about using me to get out of his school work. When the day finally passed I was exhausted I wanted to leave but also wanted some answer from Niti, she's not one to hide things from me.

"I'm going over to Niti's," I tell daddy once the school was over, he looks at me and then at Niti before replying.

"Sure, just stay out of the wood," he says.

We get into her car and take off toward her place, we did pass to the grocery store and got tons of snacks and ice cream before making it to her house. It was the first time I went to her place, her mother was home, her head did snap up when she saw me walking in, she bowed her for me and called me "Luna".

I blushed and mumbled a hello before Niti dragged me to her room, we sat on the floor with all our snacks and she began her explanation.

"What does Luna mean?" was my first question.

"Luna is you, the mate of the alpha" she explains.

"How do I smell?" I ask her.

"Like your mate, you always smell like the more dominant one. Vic has been marking you since day one but now you smell totally like him"

"Mark me?" I ask.

"Yes leave his scent on you so other wolves wouldn't get close to you" she explains, possessive much.

"Also I should warn you, all wolves are extremely possessive that includes our alpha Luna," she says the last word with a bow.

"Why did you bow?" I say worried.

"Respect girl. You deserve respect" she adds with a wink, I don't think that's very respectful.

(A bit more explanation about the wolves of my story, PS, Niti is a real person she's my friend if u see this Hey girl heheh :P. Don't forget to vote what do u think so far?)

21-Smoking.

S ophia POV.

Thank god I had Niti, she explained things to me, I did come home and roasted my so-called daddy for extra information, he explained a bit more about being Luna, about why people would bow or nod when they see me. I'm the alpha mate, he's the head of the pack, which includes lots of people, like most of the town and we're not even the biggest pack around, we have neighbors, some of them are known to be very aggressive, it's why he doesn't want me to wander around the woods.

"Would people hate me for not being a wolf?" I asked him worried since I can't change like him.

"No it's up to the more dominant one to be the alpha and he or she has to be able to shift, the Luna is more delicate and can be human" he explains.

"What about being little," I ask, do I have to give up on being a little?

"No princess, lots of alpha are into BDSM, in all its shapes and forms," he says again with a wink.

"What if I'm a bad Luna?" I say worried again.

"You can never be a bad Luna, you're my perfect mate" was his answer with a kiss to my lips, the kiss did the trick since I forgot my next question then.

That was last week, now people know who I am, they don't turn their heads when I pass, they don't jump or whisper about me being Luna, I guess they just got used to me being me. I was also getting more used to having a daddy and my brothers, they were fun to have around, they'd mess with daddy with me, but they won't share the punishment. I'd get a timeout or no candy for the day while they got away with being naught, and I thought we were in that together.

Today was a Saturday, a day we spend going out, playing with daddy's wolfie or just with Niti, but this day was different. I woke up with daddy as I did every day, we've been sleeping in the same bed ever since I accepted him, I can't and won't fall asleep unless he's there. He said it's part of our bond, we need to be together or be close, we can spend only so much time away from each other before his wolf goes crazy and come searching for me.

I woke up before him and tried to leave the bed but he had a firm hold on my waist keeping me in place, what if I needed to pee, then what! Possessive wolves, I think to myself, I try to shake him awake and slip out of his arms but to no use, I'm stuck here until he wakes up.

When he finally woke up, he let me go and I jumped to the bathroom needing to pee, when I got back Vic wasn't in bed, I went to search for him, he never leaves the house without telling me first. I sent him a message through our bond asking where he is but there was no response, I went downstairs and went to ask my brothers where he went.

"Hey, Adam have you seen Victor?" I ask.

"Still with the ugly twin baby sis?" Adam asks with a smirk.

"Not funny he's not answering me," I say with a pout.

"Oh he went with dad and Alvin to some pack business, they'll be back later," he says.

"Ohhh" I replied disappointed, why did he tell me before he left, why isn't he replying through our bond.

I was in a bad mood the whole day, I was so mad that I refused to talk to anyone, not even Sammy who tried to talk to me or make me smile. He's my sweetest brother for sure but with my bad mood, even he couldn't make me feel better. I was sitting in the corner of the porch just hiding from everyone else, I saw Adam come out to the porch he had cigarettes, I saw him light one and smoke it, he didn't notice me sitting in the corner, I stayed quiet just watching him, I had no idea he smoked, I know some people do it for fun and others when they are mad.

I saw Adam hide the cigarette pack outside in the porch, does he smoke in secret? That made me giggle in secret, of course, he left the cigarette in their hiding place and went back inside, that gave me my chance. I was feeling low the whole day maybe this would help, I walk quietly toward his hiding place and pick one cigarette and the lighter.

I took it and moved away from the porch not to get caught, I moved toward the woods, I'm not supposed to go there alone but I'm still close to the house meaning it's okay. I placed the cigarette in my mouth and tried to turn it on, I took a breath from the cigarette but it burned my nostrils and made me cough. Why would they do that, who smoke this for fun, I took another breath from it, I started to cough again, this wasn't working at all.

I was about to throw it out on the ground when I saw a wolf coming toward my side, a brown wolf with green eyes while growling I knew this wolf, he's going to kill me.

(Thank you to everyone who gave me suggestions, I will use them in the chaps to come. it's 2:05 am for now, Will see you tomorrow guys. Don't forget to vote and comment, love you)

22-Smoking kills.

Victor POV.

I woke up happily with my little in my hands, she was squirming around but I didn't want to let her go. I wanted to keep her in my hands forver, I knew she needed to pee, she didn't have to say it, but she was so focused on that feeling that she sent me the message through our bond.

She went to the bathroom and that's when everything went downhill, I was summoned by my alpha, not called down, summoned meaning I can't say no to him, I had to obey.

I made it to my father, who's still our current alpha office, I saw Alvin there too with a big scowl on his face, he hates this as much as me. Call us nicely and we'll be there, force us out of bed and you'll have one grumpy alpha and his jerk beta on your hands.

Couldn't you like call? Send a message? Sent Sammy to get me? Alvin asks, he just broke my bad mood, that guy seriously hate this. He said he'll only pledge to be my beta officially if I swear never to summon him ever.

"This couldn't wait let's go" my father says, he wasn't joking at all, he moved out of his office while we were both still in our pajamas.

"Wait where?" I ask him, he snaps at me and nod towards the outside. We move after him, he shifts to his wolf form and we do the same taking after my father. He starts running toward the edge of our territory, we move after him and saw rogues!

Rogues are wolves who found no mate, who lost their mates, their wolves takes over. There's no redemption, not even the moon goddess could save them anymore, some are just evil spirits, evil exist everywhere.

They own no lands, they own no human form, they move from one territory to another just spreading violence. And now they are in ours, it's why we always have patrols for the edges of our territory, it's why we keep an eye on who comes in.

They must have slipped through our guards, we went on and started fighting, I felt Sophia searching and calling for me, but knowing she's okay and safe at home I blocked her. I blocked our bond, the more dominant wolf can do that, we can read our mate feelings, and block ours, it's a way to keep them safe and happy.

The fight took around an hour before every rogues was dead, we shifted back and helped our hurt ones, this was going to be a busy day, from calming scared wolves, helping hurt ones and securing our borders again, the day have passed.

I opened my bond with Sophia the second I knew I was done for today, I could feel how upset she is, I'll make it up for her. She doesn't really understand much yet from our life or what being an alpha means yet, but I didn't want to scare or overwhelm her.

I walked toward our backyard slowly, I could smell cigarettes, it's one of my twin bad habits, I warned him that one day it'll land his ass in troubles. His answer was it's not going to kill him, then I heard some coughing, I looked ahead and saw Sophia! Standing with a cigarette in her hand she took another blow from it, coughed badly then threw it on the ground.

My twin was wrong smoking does kill, since I'm killing him tonight. Sophia turns and saw me coming, I couldn't help but growl she's in deep troubles, I nudge her toward the house, she tries to talk but I growl again, even knowing she's feeling guilty for what she did a good punishment is coming her way.

I stayed in my wolf form since my human clothes had blood all over them, I walked her toward my room, our room now.

"Corner" I growl through our bond making her run and obeying.

I shift back and get some random clothes before heading to the bathroom, making sure she won't see the bloody clothes, I change quickly and move back outside in human form now.

I walk toward her, she was standing in the corner, her back to me and trembling, she knew she messed up.

"Explain" I say turning her around."I was upset...I wanted to try... I'll never try it again" she stutters her excuses quickly.

I had now both hands against the wall locking her between my body and the wall. She was on the verge of crying when something snaps in her, I felt her mood shifting from a sad guilty one to pure anger.

"You left me! Without saying any words, I called you but you ignored me!" She accuse me.

I open my mouth to reply but she beats me to it, she raise her finger now, pushing my chest while scolding me.

"This is all your fault, you left without telling me!" She says and few angry tears make their way down her face, she tries to wipe the tear away but I saw it, she's right I did mess up too here.

"I'm sorry baby girl, but I had something to do" I say trying to keep the rogues out of our conversation.

"Nuu! You left me alone the whole day" she accuse again with tears now going freely down her face. Somehow our situation changes from me being mad at her to me hugging her close trying to comfort her, I shouldn't have left her like that.

"I'm sorry baby, promise I'll never ignore you again" I say genuinely. "Missed you daddy. Smoking is yuky, pwomise never again" she says and that's all I needed to know.

(1:10 am. Hehhehe, what do you think? Don't forget to vote, also feel free to message me, I always reply...once I'm awake hehhe. Luve u)

23-Period.

Victor POV.

I had to make it up for Sophia, extra cuddles and some explanation about where I was, I had to tell her about the rogue. She paled when she knew there are some people who go crazy, that there are some mean people, wolves out there. But she needs to know, it's why I'm always worried about her, I want her to know about the danger that lurks outside.

That wasn't my smartest move, she got scared, she gets closer to me crying, I didn't mean to scare her! I just meant to inform her about everything that happened but she went into her headspace and started crying.

"Daddy meany wolfie!" she says between her sobs, what am I supposed to do now, I just hugged her close, she cuddled closer to my neck. It's a comforting position for a little, to have direct access to her mate's neck, a sign of submission between any other two wolves, but for us, it's a sign of love.

"Daddy will kick any mean wolfie butt don't worry pumpkin," I tell her still trying to comfort the crying mess, it's when I felt her start sucking on my neck, she's gonna leave a mark if she keeps doing that, but that's okay with me. A sign of that I'm taken, my wolf love it, he loves everything about our little mate.

She stayed in the position until she fell asleep, I knew she was asleep because her sucking turned to a snoring voice, her body went more relax in my hands, I sighed in relief. I closed my eyes and tried to slip Sophi down a little, but she whined and went back to bury her face in my neck.

I let her be and went to sleep, I woke up to her whining in my hands again, she was pushing herself out of my hands. I let her go and she ran to the bathroom, it's when I heard her scream, I didn't think, I went and walked in on her making sure she's okay, she screamed again and closed her legs quickly.

"Daddy get out" she says in an angry voice.

"What's wrong? why did you scream?" I ask her still worried.

"Nuuu get out!" she says in a meaner voice now.

"Lose the attitude little one" I scold her making her look down and whine.

"Now tell me what's wrong?" I ask her again in a firm voice.

"gomypewid" she mumbles, I don't understand what she said, I ask her to repeat.

"Daddy....." she whines, I wasn't going to let this pass until she tells me what's wrong.

"Fiiiineee!!" she says in a whiny voice before adding in a whisper "I just got my period"

"Ohh babyyy" I say not sure what to do now, I live with three brothers and a dad, I had no idea what to do for a girl at that time of the month.

"Can you get me some pad, I don't have any. But mom should have some" she says in a low voice.

I remind myself I'm just doing this for my mate, plus Anna is my step-mother, it should be okay to ask her for that, I think to myself before heading to her's and my father room. I knock on the door and wait for a reply, dad opens the door, I blush, my baby just made me blush!

"I need Anna," I tell my dad.

"Good morning to you too son, come in" he says.

"Uhhh...Anna...Sophia is in that time of the month" I say in frustration, the thing we do for love.

"Ohh, is she okay?" Anna asks.

"She just needs some...." I tell her hoping she'll get it, thankfully she got it and went and came back with a pink box, I took it with a thank you before going back to my bathroom and handing it to Sophia.

I came back outside and waited for her, we'll skip school today, my baby isn't well and I'm not taking her anywhere when she's not okay. When she came out, I wrapped my baby in a blanket like a burrito, gave her the teddy bear that sleeps with us every night. I sat with her in bed unsure of what to do but hold her, rub her back in a calming way and let bury her head in my neck.

"You okay baby?" I ask her.

"Uh-Uh, my tummy huwt" she tells me.

"I'm sorry babyyy, what can daddy do to make you feel better?" I ask desperate, maybe I should just go ask anna for help right now.

"Howd me" she says, I do just that holding her close to me.

This is going to be a long day, but I had no idea what to do for her right now but hold her until she feels better.

(Thank you for the idea suggestion. Don't forget to vote and comment. It's only 11:47, but I need to sleep ealry tonight)

24-Cuddles&Chocolate.

S ophia POV.

My cramps got worse, they are always bad, even after my nap, daddy had me wrapped in a blanket like a burrito, to keep me warm but my stomach still hurt badly. I cried out again in pain when another strong cramp hit me, daddy pulled me even closer to him.

"What do you want me to do little one? Tell daddy what to do to make you feel better," he says, I just shrug, I don't know what to do, usually, the pain would just go on its own.

Daddy just rubbed my back, over and over again trying to make me feel better, it did but not for much, maybe I should ask daddy for a pain killer, but little Sophie hates medicine. Usually, I'd regress when in pain, just like now, daddy tried to move out of the bed but I cried tried to pull him back to bed. I didn't want him to leave, he told me he'll be back in a second, with a big pout I let him go for now.

He left the room for about ten minutes before he came back with supplies, he had a sippy cup for me with warm tea, a hot water pad, and chocolate. I smiled at that, how did he do so well? He handed me the tea first, unwrapping me from my blanket, placing the hot water bottle on my stomach before wrapping me back in my burrito blanket again.

I took few sips of the tea while he pulled me back into his lap, he opened my chocolate bar and let me have small bites slowly, all this did make me feel better now. I enjoyed my cuddle session, once my tea and chocolate were over, I went back to sucking on daddy's neck happily, it's the best place to be in.

"Sophie" daddy says trying to pull me away from his neck.

"Little one, let daddy's neck go" he says through our bond, I was surprised, forgetting that we now share this connection. I let him go and pull back a pout, he smiled at me and slipped something inside my mouth.

"What's that?" I ask him back through our bond again, he smiles at me and makes sure it's still in my mouth, I was really enjoying this feeling.

"It's your paci honey," he says explaining to me, I knew littles use these things sometimes, but this is my first time ever trying it.

"How about we watch a movie?" he asks me and I nod my head quickly yes, I would love to have a movie and cuddling time.

He turns on, Moana for us, I cuddled closer to him, my head was buried in his neck again but this time I didn't suck on his neck, instead, I sucked on my paci watching Moana and giggling. He even smiled at the songs, rubbed my back and stomach helping me feel better, as the movie went, I might have taken another nap on his shoulder.

I woke up to daddy's phone vibrating, he got his phone out, and clicked on it, he probably thought I'm still sleeping, while I made sure not to move or make a sound, he was messaging, Niti!

This got me to jump up in his hands and look at the phone, I tried to take the phone from his hand but he wouldn't give it back.

"Daddy!" I say in a whiny voice, wanting to know why he was messaging my friend.

"Sophie, honey you don't need to see it" he says but I was extremely mad now and wanted to know now.

"Give me!" I say in a pouty voice.

"Sophia, don't yell" he warns me.

"Why were you messaging Niti! My friend" I ask him still angry.

"Jealous little one?" he asks with a smirk, I wasn't joking or playing, I pulled one of his moves and opened my hand for the phone.

"You know I'm her alpha, I got every right to message one of my pack members," he says handing me it.

I opened the messages and saw him asking my friend about what to do for the Luna, aka me, when in my period. I couldn't help but giggle at that, poor daddy, he wanted to know how to help me, Niti is the one who told him about the tea, chocolate, and hot water pad.

"I'm only your little one, no being jealous, ever" he whispers in my ear.

"Sowwy daddy" I say getting back into my little space, it was really wrong to be jealous of my own best friend, but I just acted out without even thinking.

"It's okay baby girl, now you know I'm yours and only yours as you are mine. Never forget that" he assures me making me smile and cuddle closer to him ready for another movie and more chocolate.

(Thank you and Lulu for the help. I'm bored so early chap. It's 11:22pm don't forget to vote please)

25-Painters.

Sophia POV.

I was bored, seriously bored, I was done from my period thankfully, daddy took good care of me until it passed. He even gave me a very warm bath when it was over, I whined at being washed, but he wouldn't budge. He carried me to the bathroom and filled the bath with hot water for me, I sat on the counter trying to talk him out of it.

"Don't make it too hot" I whine.

"It's not" he replies still not looking back at me.

"Then don't make it too cold," I say with a pout.

"I know princess don't worry," he says ignoring all my objections.

He came and carried me off the counter, it's not the bath I'm against, it's the fact that this is the first time he'll ever bath me. With red cheeks and a beating heart of a thousand beats a minute, he sat me inside the bath naked. I'll give it to him, he didn't even look, his eyes were on my face the whole time, thankfully he got bubbles filling the tub for me to hide under them.

Having my hair being massaged by him was one of the best feelings in the world after he was done, and I was relaxed. He picked me out of the bath with a big fluffy towel wrapped around me, he helped me get dressed quickly and even brushed my white locks.

He had some new clothes for me, mostly onesies, skirts with high knee socks, and even a shirt that says "Daddy's girl", possessive much I asked him when I saw the shirt, but I still had a big smile on my face.

That was last week, this morning daddy said he's busy, he and Alvin had work. I founded out that Alvin is the Beta, he's next in charge after daddy, he can't order me around since I'm luna, but as my older brother, he said I'll have to do as asked. Not fair in my eyes but I wasn't about to have a fight with him over that, he never asks me to do anything, until today, daddy have already left, that's when Alvin came into the entertainment room where I and Sammy were having a Nintendo match.

"I want you both to stay inside today," he says before leaving.

"Why?" I ask right away while Sammy just shrugged.

"Cause I said so Sophia, stay inside," he says in a firmer voice before leaving.

I turned to Sammy but he just shrugged and said it's for our own safety, I did call daddy through our bond, he said to obey Alvin's orders and not go out today. Now we're back to being bored, really bored. I wanted to do something and little me was taking over due to boredom, everyone was out but me and Sammy.

"Sammy I'm bored," I tell him.

"Wanna do something new?" he asks and I nod yes.

"Adam has painting supplies, wanna play?" he asks and I nod yes, I'd love to paint.

"But we won't draw on papers," he says, I look at him with confusion.

"Where then?" I ask him.

"Do you wanna try face paint? I can make you a wolf" he says and I nod yes happily, I can be like daddy now.

He drags me toward Adam's room, it was the opposite of daddy's room, they are twins from the outside but they aren't the same on the inside. His room had dark colors, books, random paintings, and just some mess around here and there.

Sammy knew what he was looking for as he went straight to one of Adam's drawers and got the painting tubes out, they looked expensive, maybe we shouldn't play with them but I was so bored and Alvin had us locked in.

"Sit down," Sammy said and started to paint my face with random brushes, using different colors, he had some paint dripping on his clothes and mine, his hands were now filthy but this was so much fun. He told me he's done and I ran toward the mirror to see, he painted my whole face grey, before adding whiskers, and ears and shading my face. I really looked like a wolf, not a great one, but now I look like daddy.

"Now you do me," he says handing me the paints making a big mess.

"What do you want me to draw?" I ask him, I didn't have much talent when it came to drawing.

"Cat please," he says and I try, well I tried my best but I didn't do the best job in the world.

I tried to paint his face, I did a white base and added just whiskers to his cheeks, I had no talent to do much more.

We were giggling happily at what we did, it's how most of our day passed.

(What do you think would happen next? I'll be back in an hour with coffee hehehe)

26-Brother Fury.

S ophia POV.

I should've known that Adam would have our heart out for messing with his stuff, we really should've known better but sadly we didn't. Once he came in, he came in his room and saw his things, well the remaining of our playing session. The first reaction was to growl at us both, Sammy frowned and took a step back showing his neck, I didn't know what to do now but I was scared.

"Sophie" Sammy whispers holding my hand, Adam's eyes flashed black, he was looking at us with anger, he took a deep breath probably trying not to kill us yet. The second Adam closed his eyes Sammy took off with me behind him, we only had a head start before we heard Adam yelling at our heels.

"Samuel! Sophia! Come back here you two brats" Adam yells at us, we don't stop or go back, he'd kill us if we do.

We take off outside of the house running, we kept running until we made it to the wood, I was scared now. My heart was beating like crazy, my hands were sweating, and I was breathing quickly to keep up with all the running we're doing.

"Sophia are you okay?" I heard daddy asks through our bond.

"Nu...daddy come back." I tell him feeling hot tears going down my face, I was scared now, Adam might be my daddy's twin but right now he's scaring me, Luna or not I wanted my daddy now.

"I'm on my way" he says, we stayed hidden in the wood until daddy came, he was still in wolf form when I jumped on top of him scared, he hugged me in his wolf form, nuzzling my neck with his scout.

Once I calmed down I noticed daddy isn't alone there's another wolf with him, I looked at him trying to guess who that is, until I decided that must be Alvin.

"Good job baby, that Alvin" daddy praises me making me smile. Alvin looked at Sammy who was hiding away from everyone, they could clearly see our painted faces. Daddy moved away and shifted to his human form before coming back and hugging me in his human hands now.

"What happened Sophia?" he asks and I look down, now that he's here, I don't feel like telling him what happened.

"Sammy come here before I get your butt" Alvin warns him.

Sammy went toward Alvin looking down with tears going down his face, Alvin lifted his face looking at the paint and it's all it took for him to get what happened.

"You messed with Adams paints?" he asks with a growl, Sammy gulps, and nods.

"Ohh baby why did you do that?" daddy asks me with a shake to his head.

"Did he kill you two or did you get away?" Alvin asks.

"We ran away" I mumble.

We were dragged to the house, well I was carried while Sammy was holding Alvin's hand and staying one step behind. Once we made it there Adam was sitting on the porch smoking, he didn't look any less mad now than he did when we got away from him.

"These two have something to tell you, and I'll pay for your supplies," Alvin says giving Sammy a push.

"I'm sorry Adam" Sammy says still keeping his head down.

"Grrrr" was Adam's reply, it's when Alvin got in the middle, he pulled Sammy back behind him.

"Drop it, Adam, I'll punish him," Alvin says making Sammy whimper.

"Your turn Sophia" daddy says through our bond, I went toward Adam still holding my daddy's hand.

"I'm sorry Adam, I'll never touch your things again" I must have been forgiven since he only nodded to me before going back to sit and smoke. Daddy dragged us to our room, he made me stand in the corner, nose into the wall, he left me there for fifteen minutes before I was allowed to come out again.

"Why is Adam so mad?" I asked him while he washed my face.

"He doesn't like people to touch his supplies baby girl, and it's not polite to touch others stuff or go into their room without permission," he says scolding me.

"I'm sorry daddy, we were just bored and Alvin said no going out" I say with a big pout.

"No going out cause it wasn't safe for you" he says and I nod my head.

"And just play with Sammy or watch TV princess no touching others stuff," he says I just nod my head yes, I knew what I did was wrong now.

"I'm sorry daddy" I tell him.

"You'll have to say sorry to Adam, not me" he says and I nod, I'll have to take Sammy with me for support and help.

27-Family Love.

I didn't dare to go to Adam right away, I waited for him until he calmed down fully, also daddy said that Sammy was in deep troubles with Alvin for what he did, he knew not to mess with Adam paint supplies.

"Is Sammy a little?" I asked him wondering.

"Uhh... I don't know baby. Sammy would probably have a more dominant mate than him, but I don't know if he'll be a little" daddy explains.

"Would he have a daddy like me?" I ask excited for him, having a daddy is so much fun.

"Sophia, I don't know honey, we'll have to wait and see," he says, my curiosity wasn't satisfied yet.

"What if he gets a mommy? Are mommies better or daddies?" I ask him again.

"Sophia!" he says with a yelp.

"What if I had a mommy, that would be so sad you won't have a princess then," I say.

"Shut it little one," daddy says sticking a paci in my mouth, that made me pout but I still took it sucking on it angrily.

I closed my eyes and decided to take a nap, I was warm and cuddly in daddy's arm, I fell asleep happily there. When I woke up I was still cuddled in his hands, face buried in his neck and both hands fisted into his shirt making sure he won't take off while I'm asleep.

"Had a nice nap little one?" he asks and I nod rubbing my eyes with my fist, he took my fist asway taking at me. I whined at that but he just carried me out of the bed and into the bathroom, he started to wash my face with a wet towel taking off the paint.

Once my face was clean he let me go, he said it's time to go make amends with Adam, I went to Sammy's room but found no one. I went back to ours and asked daddy about him, he said he'll be in Alvin's room, as expected he was there, just sleeping on the bed alone.

"You okay?" I ask and he just shrug.

"Did Alvin do anything to you?" I ask worried about him, he didn't look happy.

"Forget it Sophia what do you want?" he says, maybe Alvin punished him too badly.

"Sammy wanna go make it up for Adam?" I ask him, he came up from the bed and nodded.

"Maybe we should take cookies too" I suggest and he just nods.

We moved to the kitchen and got a plate filled with cookies before we went upstairs to Adam's room, this time we knocked and waited for him to open the door and invite us in, he wasn't as mad as he was before.

"We got cookies," I tell him handing him the plate.

"Come in" he says taking the plate and taking a seat on his bed, we sat next to him, he started to eat the cookies while we just sat there looking at him not knowing what to say next. Sammy was just looking down at his lap looking miserable, I smiled at Adam but he was still eating the cookies.

"You got anything else for me?" he asks.

"Uhh...we're sorry?" I say, not knowing what to say.

"Sowwy Adam" Sammy says, maybe he's really a little.

"Come here you two" Adam says, opening his hands for us.

I went to one side of Adam while Sammy went to the other side, he hugged both of us close to him, we cuddled closer to him. I was grateful he's not mad at us anymore, my face went to Adam's neck, he smells differently from daddy, I can tell the difference between them right away now, now but they do smell differently.

"Keep it down little sis" Adam says moving my face away from his neck.

"Why?" I ask him not understanding why not. He just looks at me like I should know the answer.

"Daddy let me" I say with a big pout.

"That's because you're his mate Sophia, I'm not gonna submit to you" he says.

"Huh?" I say confused.

"He really didn't explain much to you?" he says with a sigh.

"Cuddling in the neck is only for mates or when you are more dominant," Adam explains, my mouth fell open with an oh shape, I didn't know that.

"What else?" I ask.

"You smell like Victor" Sammy this time says pulling up from Adam's chest.

"Nu I smell like me" I reply with a pout.

"No, you smell like Victor with just tiny bit of you" Sammy replies with a giggle. I turn to Adam for assurance.

"You do, you smell like your dominant mate little one, and he carries your smell too" he explain.

"Anything else?" I ask again.

"I guess you're good to go" Adam replies pulling my head back down on his chest playing with my hair.

28-Match.

Victor POV.

We had a basketball match today, we still go to school, we go every day, we only skipped few days when my baby girl had her period, then they had their paint accident on Saturday, she and Sammy were both extremely quiet Sunday. I knew that Alvin spanked Sammy for what he did, he'd been told off before about touching my twin paint supplies, maybe Sophie is right, Sammy is a little, he had some little treats in him for sure.

Today's Tuesday, we have a match today in the afternoon, Sophie said she wanna watch it, she was extremely excited, I'd say more excited than us. She was sitting in my lap this morning sharing our, well my morning coffee, she was too overactive to have one but still, she took few sips of my coffee while eating our breakfast together.

After our breakfast we got on the back of my motorcycle and headed toward the school she kept yelling to me to go faster, faster, but I didn't obey her much, I did speed up just a little bit. Once we made it to school, I helped her down my motorcycle, held her hand while we walked in, she saw her friend Niti and tried to run over to the girl.

"Daddyyy!" she whined trying to get away from me but I wouldn't let her go still holding her tight, she looks at me with confusion.

"Take it easy little one, no getting in trouble," I say knowing that she's overly excited today.

"Wes...wes...pwomise" she says in her little voice, I knew she was going to get herself into some kind of trouble or another.

I've let her go with a warning, calling Kyle right away, asking him not to let the little one out of his sight today. He said yes with a joke, saying he'll keep me updated on anything she does today.

I went to my classes as usual along with Adam, my brother who had some interesting things to tell me about my little girl and her curious questions.

"How come you never explained to her about the neck submission?" he asks.

"She likes to sleep in my neck and didn't need to know." I explain to him, if I told her about that she might decide to stop sleeping in my neck, and I loved when she did that.

"Whatever you say boss" Adam replied with a smirk.

"Did you have to be that hard on Sammy?" I ask him, we didn't have a chance to sit down and talk, well until now, being mated and alpha is taking lot of my time.

"He knows better, if Alvin didn't punished him I would" my twin replies. "Never touch Sammy" I replied between gritted teeth, using a bit of my alpha aura, that was an order.

"Yes,alpha" he replies, I felt bad for forcing something on him but it had to be done.

Our day passed quietly until lunch and my baby girl came, she didn't want to eat busy talking with her friend. I had to force her to shut it and eat, that made her eat with a big pout but at least she had some food down her throat.

"Bye Vic" she said as soon as lunch ended getting away from me since I'm the bad guy who made her eat. I held her back and kissed her on the mouth, not really caring that we are at school, she's my mate and half of this town is made up from pack member.

This got her to blush and forget all about her being mad at me, she ran toward Niti gushing about how cute I am, girls. The day finally passed and it was time for the match, a rumor around the school was going on about a party in the woods when we win.

I had Sammy to bring Sophia down to her seat with the rest of the team before he went back toward his friends, she's staying where I can see her even during the match, call me possessive, look how much I don't care.

The match began and the whole school was cheering for us, the only voice ai heard was Sophia, she was wishing me luck through our bond. I turned to smile at her before the game started, we won, of course we did.

I earned a big kiss afterwards,I told her to wait for me until I get my stuff, I can shower at home and celebrate with ice cream with my mate. When I came back out running I didn't see her, not at the stadium, outside, next to my bike, with one of my brothers. She just disappeared.

(What do u think happened? I'll be back tomorrow. Good night people it's 12:14am for me)

29-Party rumor.

S ophia POV.

There's a rumor about a party later tonight, it's in the wood only the wolves know where it is. Me being their new Luna, I never loved my new title until now, me being their Luna I was invited in with them, saying I have to come.

When Kyle heard about that he said to forget it, Victor would skin him alive if I even think about going.

"Why not?" I ask with a big pout. "It's a werewolf party little sis, not the normal one, it's not safe for Luna to go alone" was his answer that didn't really explain much.

"Then you come with me" I tell him happily, if I need someone to come he can. "No I can't go with you Luna, I'm not the alpha and again Victor would have my heart for it," he says in explanation.

"Grrrr...you no fun" I stumped away from him dragging my bestie Niti with me, at least she's on my side right.

"Soph calms down he's right I've been to one of those parties before." She says and I'm ready to call our friendship off and beat her ass right now.

"But being a Luna there does have its advantages" she adds with one of her evil smiles, I smile back knowing I just won her on my side.

"How we do this?" I ask her, this is my first party around here, I love my daddy and brothers but they could be a bit overprotective of me.

This isn't little me who wants to go, little me ie terrified of parties, but I want to go so badly. If I don't sneak for parties now while young when would I do it, I thought to myself with a giggle.

"First don't tell the alpha anything," she says and I nod, I already figured that out, don't tell Victor.

"After today's match, we'll catch a ride with someone there. You can see the party enjoy it for a bit then we'll go back home and beg for forgiveness" she says.

"Niti!" I say in desbelif. "I've been to those parties before Luna, believe me, ten minutes are more than enough. Plus it'll take less than ten for someone to tell the alpha you are there" well when she said it this way, she does have a point.

"Okay deal," I say. "For now just act normally," she says and I nod before going to lunch with her and the boys.

We were talking about random things when daddy had enough with me and forced me to eat some food. I was ready to storm off in anger when he pulled me back for a kiss making my heart melt and my knee weak.

"That was so hot, I can't wait to find my own mate," Niti says in a dreamy voice making me giggle. "O,h no little one our love would be a bit more firmer, tone of sex, and more sex" at that I lost the smile, yeeks.

"Don't frown my mate won't be able to resist this" she adds showing off her figure with both hands making me giggle at how silly she's acting.

When the time for our plan and the match came Sammy walked me down to sit with the team, I had Kyle there with me and Adam, now I know the difference between them, I thought to myself.

I wished them all good luck before they went in, I sheared for daddy to win. He won, he did so well, I was supposed to wait for him till he's back so we can leave and that was my cue, I went out with the rest of the students and searched for Niti.

When I found her standing with the other two guys I ran toward them, we got in their car quickly and took off toward the woods.

"We're so honored to have you with us Luna," one of the guys says and I smile at him, not knowing what to say more. When Victor knows I'm here with them he'll be worse than Adam when we messed with his paint.

We almost made it to the wood when I heard daddy calling me through our bond, I froze like I was caught red-handed stealing cookies. I looked at Niti with fear, what do I do? Do I reply or not? What should I tell him?

"I don't know" Niti whisper reply too scared he'll hear her too.

That's silly but right now I'm too afraid he'll hear her too, I tried to come up with a lie, an excuse.

"Took a ride home with Niti," I say hoping he'll believe me before shutting up and going to enjoy my ten minutes before we leave.

(Good morning people, it's 10 am for me, ready for multiple updates today. Don't forget to vote)

30-Party

S ophia POV.

The party wasn't exactly what I expected, I expected people with red cups, I expected music and dancing. Instead some were in wolf form, others in human form dancing.

Everyone was sniffing everyone, there was some boose but drinking directly from the bottles, few wolves were now fighting with each others.

Suddenly, the music started, it was just music no words, I'm not good with explaining what type of music this is, but the dancing got more common, the wolves all looked up and howled. I'd want to say howling to the moon but it was still too early for the moon to come out, maybe to the sun.

Niti took my hand and started dancing with me, everyone was dancing now, you'd think beiny in the middle of the forest would give us some space between us but instead we're all rubbing against each others.

Some would bump into me take a deep breath, bow their heads and moves, my main dance partner was Niti, it was fun, I loved the dancing, I also got in with the howling rythm, every now and then they'd howl, even the one in human form.

"Aowwwwwww" I howled with them, giggling.

"You enjoying your time Luna?" Someone asks and I just jod stull happy to dance and howl with everyone else.

"Can I have this dance then?" The guy says pulling me closer to him.

"No thank you" I say pushing him away from me, he tried to pull again and I pushed him as hard as I can. He turned to his wolf form and growled at me, I growled back at him it's when he went to his wolf form.

To that I had no reply, he wasn't as big ot scary as daddy or Alvin, but he still scared me. He kept his growling and looking me straight in the eyes, I don't know what he expected me to do, I was like a dear stuck in the spot light, scared of him and frozen.

He kept growling, but I stood there not understanding, we must have stayed like that for a long time since most people are now looking at us, what's happening. Finally after so long of this staring contest the other guy bowed his head, turned on his heels and ran away toward the woods.

Everyone was quiet now, until they all broke up into howls and cheers, they were all congratulating me but on what? "What happened?" I ask Niti. "You butchered his ego Luna" she says giving me a high five.

"I did?" I ask, no one dared to get even close to me now. "Yes you just forced your dominance on him" she says. "What?" Is she for real. "The best part is that you don't even know you did, he tried to make you submit but you stood there, the more dominant wins" she says.

"But I thought I'm a submissive" I whisper to Niti, I'm a little, meaning I'm a submissive I knew that much. "But you're also Luna, you only submit to your mate. Being bonded to him gives you some of the alpha aura" well that's something for sure.

I'm so cool, I thought to myself before going back in with the dancing and howling. I didn't notice we've been here for long time, I only knew I messed up with the time when daddy called me again through our bond.

"Sophia I'm home where are you?" He asks and I panic, we should go back home now, we can't stay here and be busted.

I try to find Niti but she's not next To me anymore, she's lost somewhere in the crouds, I went on a messy searching trip not able to find her.

"Niti" I call loudly, but no answer the music got louder now, the howling wasn't fun it was scary, I was ready to go home. But Niti was my guide home, I don't know how to leave from here alone.

"You okay Luna?" A random guy asks me, I don't know who that is so I just nod yes saying I'm okay before going back to search for my friend.

I found Niti finally, I held her hand and told her I wanna go home now, daddy must be worried about me now. He's yelling in my head asking where I am, the music stopped all the suden.

Loud howls could be heard but not the howls we've been doing this whole time, these were different, these sounded louder, meaner.

What did I get myself into...

(Uh-oh what's gonna happen now? Don't forget yo vote and comment)

31-Naughty girl.

Victor POV.

    I couldn't find her, she's not in the school, parking lot, with my brothers, I was losing it, where the hell is that naughty little girl.

I called her through our bond asking where she went! She said she had a ride home with her friend, it's not usual for her to do anything like that. She usually waits for me and we'll leave together, never alone and never in this secret way.

I was worried about her now, if she said she's going home then I shoulf go home too. I got on my bike and took off toward the house.

The rest of the pack and teammate said they want to go to this party. It's not uncommon to have parties in the woods, sometimes my family would join and others not. They needed a permission to do this party and it was granted, but I didn't plan on going there too.

When I got home I went to our room but didn't find Sophia there, I went to her old bedroom and still nothing. I started searching for her again, I ran through the house searching for my baby, her scent wasn't as prominent as it should be if she came by.

But I kept telling myself she might just be somewhere else in the house. My search took me toward the backyard, the woods and still no little one. I asked Sammy her partner in crime if they were up to anything and he said no. Adam was with me the whole time, Alvin was busy on patrols, that only left Kyle.

"Kyle sophia didn't come home yet, do you know where she is?" I ask him worried about hrr.

"No haven't seen her since school" he replies. "Did she say anything back at school? She was overactive the whole day" I ask again, she wasn't in her little space, I worried more about big Sophia then little Sophia when it came to her missbehaving. The worse little Sophie can do is eat cookies without my permission but big Sophia could do much worse then that.

"No..." Kyle says but he seems to be thinking about something, he had this look on his face that says guilty.

"Kyle" I ask. "Okay fine!! She asked about the party, I told her she can't go! And that you'll have my heart out if I take her there" he says, I knew he wasn't lying right now, his eyes and voice were telling the truth but right now I knew where my baby went!

Kyle was right, I would have anyone's heart for taking here there, but I'll have the princess bum-bum for what she did. Lying to me, sneaking out, going to a party without my permission.

I used our bond to ask her again where she is, if she comes clean, I might take it easier on her. She didn't reply, it was then that I felt her fear, it wasn't like the time Adam scared her, this time her fear was real.

I jumped on my feet and took off running, I called my beta Alvin, he hate to be summoned but doesn't mind when we talk via our Alpha/beta bond. I asked him if he knew about anything going down but my brother didn't reply, he always replies quickly.

Now that my fear has doubled I ran faster, until I reached the meadow where the party was held. There was a mix of wolves smells and scents, some alcohol, but what scared me the most was the last scent I could identify was what scared me.

"Alpha...we...got a problem" my brother said through our bond, I knew something was wrong the second I reached here but his voice sounded weak, not a good sign.

"Where are you Alvin?" I ask him. "Had to call dad for help, I'm in the infirmary." He says makimg my heart drop.

If my strong dominant wolf brother was in the infirmary what would have happened to my baby.

"Alvin where's Sophia?" I ask but no answer.

"Alvin where's my mate" I ask him again raising my voice.

When he doesn't reply I shift back to my human side, the whole fear and emotion's are having the best of me.

"DAMN IT ALVIN WHERE THE HELL IS MY BABY?" I yell out loud and through our bond.

"I'm sorry alpha they took her" he says with an appolgetic voice.

I drop to my knees and let one long, hollow, filled with all the pain I'm feeling howl.

The rogues just took my mate.

(Action action hehehehhehe.... what's next. I'll be back later with coffee heheheh don't forget to vote)

32-Attack.

S ophia POV.

The howls got closer, they got worse, I wasn't the only one scared now. Everyone was scared, some took off running others screamed to protect the Luna! I'm the Luna!

It's then I saw some wolves walk toward us, their eyes were pure red, their teeth were sharp and showing out of their mouthes. They looked mean and evil, these must be the rogue daddy told me about, what did I get myself into.

They walked toward us in their ugly forms, they took deep breaths looking around until their eyes landed on me. Thd first guy that walked toward me, he must be their boss or something, he came toward me. Stood in front of me and took a very deep breath, he looked around but I had no idea who he's looking for.

Once he didn't find whoever he's looking for he started laughing, an evil laugh coming from him that sounded more like a dying hyena. I tried to take a step back but he growled at me making me stop right there in my track.

"Don't touch our Luna" a guy jump in front of me trying to protect me. His act of hero cost him his life, the rouge killed him, right there in front of my own eyes, he bitten him on the neck crushing his windpipe. I never saw someone die in front of me until now, I wasn't missing much, I wish I could forget that right away.

The rest of the people around here took a step away from me, this wasn't me playing with the others and holwing. It wasn't me showing off dominance without even knowing, this was real, this was dangerous.

The mean one was walking around me in circles, licking his dirty lips, growling at others and just sniffing me in general. It's then that we heard others, but these growls weren't scary. They were we are saved growls first I saw Alvin! Thank god I'm saved!

He had others with him now, he ran toward me first, the meanie guy he growled at Alvin. My brother growled back, showing off his teeth, Adam wasn't meanie looking but he was scary in his own way.

They stood nose to nose now, both growling, I wanted to take off and run I wanted to yell for my daddy but I was frozen just in place from fear. They started to fight, Alvin was on top first but then he had got hit in the shoulder, blood starting seeping out.

He didn't stop yet, he went back for the offender neck, but he cheated, hitting him again on his injured shoulder until he fell on the ground with agony.

It wasn't the only fight going here, other rogues were fighting ours, no one was looking at me, I was frozen in the middle looking at Alvin and the other one.

I knew I did the wrong thing, I should've called daddy then, I should have ran away, I should've done something. But my fear had me frozen, I saw

Alvin take another hit, more blood and finally he went stiff on the ground scaring me.

I felt hot fat tears going down my face, I wanted to call my mate now but I couldn't no matter how hard I tried to think about him I couldn't.

The rogue who was hitting my brother he pulled back they were wining the fight, he turned to his human form right in front of me.

He was dressed in rags, clothes that hardly covers anything he wasn't even able to walk properly on two feets, I thought rouges stays in their wolf form all the time but I guess wrong.

He walked toward me with pure menace, he slashed my shirt leaving long claw marks on my body before tying both my hands behind my back with my own shirt rag.

I was trembling, scared, and crying, he looked at me in the face then slapped me hard. I fell on the ground blacking out, I thought I knew fear before, but I've never felt anything even close to this.

I don't remember much of what happened next, just that I was taken away from my pack, home, family, and my daddy.

I hope my daddy can save me, I was sure of that first. But three months later, they told me they killed him, he's still an empty space in my head and heart.

If you are alive and out there, Daddy Victor please forgive me.

(Poor sophie... I'm working on next chap soon babes. Don't forget to vote)

33-Searching.

Victor POV.

I need to find her! I need to have her back in my arms, I need her, my wolf is going crazy, howling inside my brain demanding her back where she's safe, with us. I was walking back and forth, wanting to find her, the rouges took her that's all I knew, but where did they take her.

I made the whole pack search with me, every enforcer, everyone who knew how to fight, even the slightest knowledge of fighting. All those are expected to come up with me and search for their future Luna, we need to find my baby!

People who were at the party said they saw the rogues come to the party, they took the Luna and left, my brother was injured, a guy died trying to protect my girl, he deserves a salute from me. But now we need to find her, the rogues don't have a place, they are all over the place they never stay in one place but why did they take what's mine.

It's not usual for them to take a Luna? They only killed, they never abduct until now, but where would they hide her? They won't walk around with her, they'll either kill her and be over with it, or hide her somewhere.

I knew she was alive, I could feel her inside me, on my chest her name was still written in black ink, if it turns red, that means my baby is dead, or she rejected me. She never rejected me, and she's alive, our bond is dead, I tried to call her, I tried my best to tell her to come back, to ask where she is, but she wouldn't hear me.

She blocked me, she doesn't know how to block her mate, especially me, but I knew something bad happened, too bad that she blocked me either by mistake or cause of someone interfering with our connection. No one can mess with two mates' connections except the goddess, but why would she do that? Why would she take her away!

I was close to tears, but there's no resting, no stopping, we all need to search until we find her, we need her back and I need to strangle the rouge who took my baby! He's dead meat walking, once I get my hands on him.

We searched everywhere, over our land, on our territory edge, we even took permission from our neighbor's packs and searched on their territory with their enforcers staying with us to make sure we don't try anything.

We still couldn't find her, everyone knew about me searching for my baby girl, everyone knew if they even heard about rogues or where they are to just call us. We did get some random calls, we went there, we killed every rogue we saw, we called so many of them but we couldn't find my baby girl, no matter how hard we searched, now many rogues we investigate with asked them her. They all said they had no idea about the Luna, some were grateful to be killed, they wanted their life to end and be over with it.

It's been three months now, over ninety days, and no Sophia, the season has changed now, we're in the summer. Summer the days when I planned on taking Sophia swim, to have longs walks and picnics, but now she's gone.

I needed help, my wolf was going out of control, he wanted to kill, he wanted to take his revenge on everyone. Late-night he'd tell me it's all the fault of her friend, the one who took her to the party, others he'd say it's Alvin's fault, he should have died to protect his Luna.

I'd shake those ideas off, I'd tell myself it's my fault, I'm the one who should keep my baby safe, I'm the one who could help her, I'm the one who should be blamed.

I cried again, I wasn't ashamed to cry anymore, I needed help, I needed my baby, anyone who got a word on her. They could ask for my soul and I'll give it but I need her, I need her so badly. I hugged her teddy and cried again, today we are home but tomorrow we are going after another lead, I'll keep searching for you my baby Sophia, never think that daddy is giving up on you....never baby girl.

34-Rescue Mission.

V ictor POV.

I've had enough, we're getting my baby back before I lose it and go rogue before I kill my own siblings, my own pack. I can't let that happens, I'm calling everyone and anyone who's in alliance with us, especially an alpha next door, she's one the meanest alpha's ever alive. She's known for torturing rogues, she accepted to help us, to torture some of her rogues, and ask about my Luna.

But who knew that she could do it, that it worked, that finally, she got some information, that she knows where my baby is. Four months later and finally we have a lead. The rogue who took her is dead, he died but no one knew where she was, the message alone had me ripping my clothes, yelling screaming, howling my anger to the moon goddess, I was swearing at her and the skies.

"Calm down Victor! Vic please alpha!" Alvin says trying to calm me down but I couldn't I was so mad right now, I didn't even bother to read the rest of her message.

"Calm down jerk! They found her" Adam says, he might be the only one who dared to call me a jerk right now. He's right I'm acting like now right now.

I calmed down, just enough to ask him where she is, he said the message says it's between three places that they might have her hidden. In the last month, all the rogues who took her are dead, rogues don't live long to start with, they either kill each other or get killed, some even commit suicide to simply be over with the pain of having no mate.

We got ready, us, all the alleys I could find, and went toward the first space in the list, the alpha even sent me some of her own men. She's a damn good fighter, matless, God helps us if she goes rogue, she'd kill everyone without a second glance.

The first place she told us about was a cave, a simple cave is hidden in the mountain but except for few rogues that I was more than happy to kill there was no one else. We moved to the next place, it was an abandoned house, empty, not a trace to my baby, the final place happened to be a warehouse.

"Empty! Empty again!" I yell! Angry, now I can't find her, I'll never find her now, even with all the help with searching for her for over four months and we still can't find her.

"Why Would You Do That To Me!!!" I yelled at the goddess, why wouldn't she give me what's mine again! Why would she torture me so badly.

"Let me go rogue...let me die..." I say openly sobbing not caring about anything anymore, kill me and be over with it.

"Victor..." my brother says.

"I can't anymore...." I sob heartbroken, letting one last strangled howl, filled with my own tears. I heard a howl back. One that was so feminist, one that was tired, but one that I knew, even though I never heard it before, it was my baby voice.

I took off toward that sound, this wasn't the only warehouse around here, the rogue who gave the alpha the information was wrong with the number. She's not here, she's there! I'm coming for you little one, I call through our dead bond, she must be alive, she must survive for me.

When I found her she was in a warehouse alone, she was locked inside a cage, her clothes were the same ones she had on her the day she was taken, she was extremely thin now, her white hair was black with how dirty it is. She looked at me with a sad smile before fainting again, I ran toward her and broke the stupid cage taking her into my arms, she's back in my hands and safe.

I tried to use our bond but it still wasn't working I didn't understand what's wrong with our bond, but we'll fix it once we are back at safety. I checked her neck for any bite marks, she had few which made me growl with anger, they dared to touch what's mine! It can all wait until we are back home, back to when I can make sure she's safe.

It was dark now, we've been all over the place searching for her, few rogues could go such long distances even while holding a girl with them.

I took her home, it was a full day drive, she simply slept, she slept until we made it home. She slept while the doctor checked on her, she slept when I washed her when I made sure her white hair is once again white.

"What's wrong with her doctor?" I asked our pack doctor, my heartbreaking seeing my baby angel still sleeping.

"They tried to claim her, she refused their bite, it might have interfered with your bond. That happened months ago, there's nothing wrong with her physically. She'll wake up when she's ready" the doctor says and I thank him for his time simply sitting next to her and waiting for my baby to be back where she belongs in my arms.

35-Recovery.

Sophia POV.

They took me, he tried to bite me the second I blacked out, now I remember everything, he tried to bite me, saying I'm his mate now. That I can't reject him again, that he's my mate now, he kept calling me Lillian, I wasn't her, but he wouldn't believe me, no matter how much I told him I'm not her, that he can't claim me because I belong to someone.

Sometimes he'd yell and tell me I'm his, others he'd just cry and begs me not to leave him, promising to be good for me. I just nodded to him too afraid, when he did bite me, it hurt me, he made my bond with Victor feel weird. I still felt daddy but I couldn't talk to him, even when I tried he can't hear me, the other guy, he stayed in his human form while talking to me and bringing me food. But others he'd go to his wolf form and scare the hell out of me, I was grateful for the cage then, he can't get to me while in his wolf form.

Days passed, and then more days passed, finally the one who had abducted me didn't come back, I stayed there alone, I tried to make my food and water to last me as long as possible. For the last week, I didn't have anything,

I was spending most of the day sleeping, too tired to wake up or even lift my head.

Then I heard a howl, not the rogues howl, it's similar to the one I heard back at home, the one we howled at the party. I decided to give this a chance I need to be saved, I lifted my head and howled back with all my strength, it was loud, too loud for my own ears. It took too much of my own strength, I fell asleep after that.

I don't remember much until I woke up in daddy's lap, my head was on his chest, a paci in my mouth, him playing with my hair. I heard other's voices, it was my brothers' voice, that made me smile they are here, I'm back.

"Daddy?" I ask through our bond, it's working now again! Finally!

"Baby you're okay?" he asks kissing my face all over with kisses making me smile, I didn't feel like talking yet.

"I missed you so much, I'm never letting you go, never ever" he says landing more kisses on my face and neck. I was too weak to actually push him away but I did enjoy his attention.

"Victor! She's our sister too! We want to see her" I hear Alvin says that got me to sit up happily wanting to see my brothers.

"Leave and be back when I'm done loving her...that would be never" daddy replied making me giggle again.

"Not fair jerk, we miss her too" Adam says, I giggle again.

"You want to see them honey?" he asks me and I nod yes, I do want to see my brothers.

"Come in." daddy says and they run inside, they run toward me trying to give me a hug, but daddy growled at them making them stay away.

"You really should've chosen me, little sis, I'm the more handsome brother," Adam says making me giggle.

"Welcome back Luna," Alvin says with a real smile, holding Sammy in his arms.

"Welcome back girl," Kyle says giving me a high five.

Finally, Sammy got close and gave me a quick hug, keeping it light so I won't be hurt. I smiled at them through my paci too happy with it to spit it out yet.

"Leave you four, I need to feed her" daddy says, I look up at him with confusion, he just smiled at me and kicked our brothers out. For food, he got a baby bottle, I looked at it with surprise, what's this about.

"You haven't eaten in so long, hard food is too much for you," he says and I nod okay maybe he does have a point.

He forced my paci out and changed it to the bottle nipple, it was weird at first but I took it happily, the warm milk made my stomach feel warm and full. I drank the whole thing, happy and full, when it was done daddy changed the bottle for my paci again helping me fall asleep on his chest.

36-Mating.

Sophia POV.

I was in my little space after I came back, we didn't go to school for more than one reason, well it was summer the school was already over and I was in no shape to go there. We both skipped, daddy took care of me with everything, it took me two weeks to be able to talk again, three weeks of being bottle-fed to be able to stomach hard food again.

But I'm better now, I'm alive and I'm back, daddy asked me to mate with him. We are already mates but make it official, to become luna and alpha, his wolf grew up so much in my absence the trauma made him even more dominant and possessive of me. The only person who get's to hug me from my siblings is Sammy, I still doubt he's a little, he'd play with me while in my little space.

I tried asking him once but he just shrugged said no, and to drop it, but now back to my mating ceremony. It's like a wedding for werewolves but he has to bite me and I'll accept him, we'll be two mated werewolves. There's also sex that would come next, Niti was extremely talkative about that part, telling me all about it, while daddy said we can not do that until I'm ready.

But I think I was ready, I wanted to have my chance with daddy in every way we can be together. There was no dress code, I could wear whatever I wanted, me and mom chose a royal blue dress, daddy approved saying it's beautiful.

The ceremony was going to happen in the woods, under the same tree that daddy told me all about the legend, about us being mates. It was a special place for us that we both agreed on, it was a romantic place that has a special place in my heart. Fred was the one who'll do the mating for us since he's our alpha, daddy, and I would be taking over after him soon.

I was dressed in my fancy dress, got my hair done with some simple make-up with mom's help, for shoes I went with flats since I wasn't that good with high heels. Everyone agreed with me on that choice, most of the pack was there too, we had a bonfire there too, a small party for the whole pack.

I stayed hidden in my mom's room away from my daddy's eyes to keep the surprise, Alvin was the one who drove us to the forest, he's the one who walked me to where daddy and the alpha were waiting for us. I smiled at daddy standing there in his tuxedo and looking at me like I'm the only person there, Alvin walked me toward them.

It was like a human wedding, except the words we said, it wasn't for sickness and for health, and the ceremony didn't end with kissing the bride.

"I Victor, take you, Sophia, as my mate, to love and protect till the goddess take me back," he says.

"I Sophia, take you, Victor, as my mate, to love and protect under the goddess moon," I say.

They were strange vows but that was all we had to do before daddy bent in to bite me, I closed my eyes scared first, he kissed my neck making me relax, licked my neck making me moan, and finally he bite me. I didn't feel any pain, it was something that made me extremely aroused, I moaned from the feeling, he smiled at me licking my neck making me close my eyes from the feeling.

Everyone cheered for us, saying their congrats, again with my possessive mate, he wouldn't let anyone get too close to me to give me hugs or congratulations, just Sammy.

"I still think he's a little," I tell him through our bond with a smile, he just smiles and shakes his head at me.

The rest of the night was passed in dancing and celebrating, this was our night, he's mine now and I'm his, now and forever.

How about Sammy? Do you think he's a little? Do you want to see his own story? Check him and see if he ends up being a little, "Forced beginnings" is his story, I'm publishing that story cover, I'll start updating it soon.

THE END.